Michele Finn Johnson's stories are populated with Catholic schoolgirls and awkward baseball players, hot ghosts and cold angels, thirsty girls, harried parents, and dead twins with bat wings. Her characters are voracious, sardonic, full of longing. Reading this book feels like watching a talented magician perform a series of dazzling tricks. *Development Times Vary* is a wild, nimble, playful, and moving book, charting, as the title promises, the unpredictable and uneven ways people, feelings, and revelations grow.

—Kim Magowan, author of *How Far I've Come*

Sharply observant children who see the people in their orbit with a bird's-eye view; teenagers who ache to be seen; lessons about ants, bats, and lunar facts; dead who tend the living; a slew of shitty boyfriends; and lust, lust, lust: These are a few of the ingredients of which Michele Finn Johnson's *Development Times Vary* is made. Wise and poignant and companionable, these are stories I wish I could send as love letters to my thirteen-year-old self and, well, my twenty-something selves and my thirty-something selves, too.

—Michelle Ross, author of *They Kept Running*

Development Times Vary serves up a brew of playfulness and consequence, of innocence and wisdom and sass. Whether a Catholic schoolgirl lost in the shuffle of adolescence, a boy haunted by the bat-ghost of his dead twin, or a fruit-fly-breeding pothead obsessed with a popular jock, the characters of Michele Finn Johnson search, struggle, make mistakes, and often learn more than they want to know. Bursting with Johnson's inimitable voice, these stories shimmer and sting.

—Jennifer Wortman, author of
This. This. This. Is. Love. Love. Love.

By turns tender, quiet, and astonishing, *Development Times Vary* contains deeply resonant tales of unraveling connections. Whether it is "School Lessons" chirping with dolphin shouts, paper football and learning cultures or "Lunar Facts," a list-style exploration of the layers that are at times bright, then waning, cyclical like the moon, Michele Finn Johnson is an author of singular voice and vivid imagination. She paints a world of characters in a small space and masterfully connects the dots between the loving and the broken in her captivating debut collection.

—Tara Isabel Zambrano, author of
Death, Desire, and Other Destinations

In *Development Times Vary*, Michele Finn Johnson delivers short stories that will stick with you for a long time. There are moments of absurdity, moments of heartbreak, moments of revelation, and more than a few bats, but what make these stories really special are the characters, each with a unique and memorable voice. This is a collection that excavates the human experience and finds hope nestled against despair, humor hiding beneath rage, heroism wrapped up in self-doubt, and love sharing space with grief. Johnson is a master of short fiction, and I can't wait to see what she writes next.

—Tiffany Quay Tyson, author of *The Past Is Never*

How can one writer have so many strange and wonderful stories living in her head? Defies the laws of physics. *Development Times Vary* is at times funny, at times deeply moving, consistently startling. You'll love living in Michele Finn Johnson's brain.

—William Haywood Henderson, author of *Augusta Locke*

In *Development Times Vary*, Michele Finn Johnson captures the pangs of young love and obsession, eerie urban legends, the foreboding elements of nature, and the thin veil between reality and the paranormal. She holds space for the full range of human experience, carrying readers along into a wonderful, expansive daydream. This is a feat of a debut.

—Christopher Gonzalez, author of *I'm Not Hungry But I Could Eat*

DEVELOPMENT TIMES VARY

Michele Finn Johnson

The 2021 Moon City Short Fiction Award

MOON CITY PRESS
Department of English
Missouri State University
901 South National Avenue
Springfield, Missouri 65897
www.moon-city-press.com

First Edition
Copyright © 2022 by Michele Finn Johnson
All rights reserved.
Published by Moon City Press, Springfield, Missouri, USA, in 2022.
Manufactured in the United States of America.

Library of Congress Cataloging-in-Publication Data

Library of Congress Control Number: 9780913785676

Johnson, Michele Finn.
Development Times Vary:

Further Library of Congress information is available upon request.

ISBN-10: 0-913785-73-3
ISBN-13: 978-0-913785-73-7

Cover designed by Shen Chen Hsieh
Interior designed by Cam Steilen
Text edited by Karen Craigo
Author Photo by Cat Hope Photography

moon city press
Department of English
Missouri State University

CONTENTS

for Karl Andrew Johnson,
forever and a day

DEVELOPMENT
TIMES VARY

SCHOOL LESSONS

HOW WE ARRIVE

The yellow buses wind through a three-mile radius of suburban streets and arrive, miraculously, at the same time each day. They usher themselves within the double yellow lines of the St. Pius X schoolyard, yielding to each other without incident. One by one, the bus doors open, and we disembark. There is no yelling, no whooping. We cluster in the areas designated for each of our grades. We stay within painted white lines.

HOW WE MOVE

Maybe it is because that is how they tell us to walk, single file—ducks waddling after the mother of all ducks, Sister Quackenpuss. Or maybe it is because they want to be able to look at the length of us, the human yarn we create stretched out across the schoolyard. Maybe it makes it easier to inspect us for flaws—improper tie knots, mismatched socks, untucked blouses. Whatever the reason, that is how we move, long and skinny and purposeful.

When they call our names it is always the same, in alphabetical order, and we chirp *Here*, and sometimes when they call my name I do not chirp loud enough, and they do not hear me, and they call my name again, and I know that I need to chirp louder. *Here.* My second *Here* is shrill—a dolphin shout—and I want to disappear.

Some people are separated because, together, they are greater than the sum of their parts. For example, Larry McCarthy + John Massimo = snot rockets and stink bombs. Cindy Appleton + Pauly Harmon = kissy kissy slobber and a prolific production of folded sheets of paper passed back and forth at Mach 2 speed. Bobby Rocco + anyone else with burgeoning testosterone = paper footballs and finger goalposts. They keep some type of matrix, they must have a matrix, and these lethal combinations—those that add up to more than Sister Quackenpuss or, God forbid, the weaker layperson, Miss Margaret, can handle—are separated.

HOW WE LEARN

The cinder block walls are lined with posters—the pyramids of Egypt, pharaohs, bars of gold lying at the feet of stone creatures. Our World Cultures teacher is Miss Margaret, and maybe it is because she doesn't wear the Quackenpuss headdress or because she doesn't purse at us with Brillo-pad lips, but we ignore Miss Margaret; we do not listen to her tales of pyramid building or live burials. We build pyramids of our own out of pencil erasers. Larry McCarthy and Cindy Appleton switch seats with John Massimo and Pauly Harmon while Miss Margaret draws a giant pulley-and-lever system on the blackboard. A wet tissue plops onto the back of my head. I turn in time to see Larry McCarthy + John Massimo laughing and Cindy Appleton + Pauly Harmon swapping spit.

Recess. They call it free time, but we are quarantined to select areas of the schoolyard. This is done by grade. The unfortunates—the first-to-third graders—are limited to the area in front of the convent. Sister Owl Eyes perches in the window of the Convent with a Bible on her lap, and no matter where you are in the schoolyard you will catch a fiery glint off her silver crucifix. You cannot truly escape Sister Owl Eyes until fourth grade when you move to the area in front of the rectory, where the priests mainly sleep and cow-snore the day away.

By someone's lapse of judgment, we eighth-graders take our recess down the hill beyond the church parking lot, out of view of the convent and the rectory and the school. We head down the hill, single file by height, and sometimes due to unpredictable laws of puberty, the people who should not be together due to laws of addition are, in fact, together, and the single file line of ducklings is loud with handmade farts and actual farts and an occasional smoke bomb.

The class matrix is disrupted when New Girl comes. She has Gee, Your Hair Smells Terrific hair and a toothy smile and a fake leg. She is in uniform, standing in front of the class, and Sister Quackenpuss looks at New Girl with an actual smile on her face as she introduces her. We are all looking at the plastic knot that is New Girl's kneecap. Sister Quackenpuss seats New Girl up front and center, then parts the room in two and has us shift our assigned seats one spot to our left or right, snaking our way to the back of the room, maintaining the original matrix except for a few unforeseen overlaps where end seats became middle seats, and now the previously isolated are in the exact middle of the room, and we can all see the trouble that is to come.

New Girl plays basketball. Her hair swings with invisible wind and still manages to land back in place. Her fake leg stops at the knee, and I sit on the bench looking at the color-perfect match of flesh and plastic. When she jumps, I cringe and hold my face in a scrunch until her feet land on the gymnasium floor in a squeak.

Miss Margaret is lenient with the bathroom passes, and sometimes I ask for one when I am bored. Today I am bored with the Revolutionary War and its stupid battles. Someone is vomiting in the stall next to me. I cannot tell who it is because we all wear the same saddle shoes. I wait in the stall until the bell rings and we both have to come out. It is Cindy Appleton. *I'm fine*, she says, but next week during the Louis and Clark lecture she is in the stall next to me vomiting again.

☾

Attendance at detention has increased since New Girl's arrival. I do not mean to blame this on New Girl. No. She is never at detention, but with the class rearrangement, Pauly Harmon is now only one seat apart from Cindy Appleton, and Cindy Appleton is right next to John Massimo, and John Massimo has abandoned his prior interest in stink bombs and wet tissue bombs and all things bomblike and has taken a bigger interest in Cindy Appleton and the training bra that she is outgrowing. John Massimo snaps Cindy Appleton's training bra and Pauly Harmon snaps the back of John Massimo's head with his World Cultures book and who could blame Miss Margaret for sending the entire row to detention when no one would admit to anything. I am in this row. I stare at John Massimo and Cindy Appleton and Pauly Harmon as I clap erasers and disappear in a plume of chalk.

All mothers are required to be Lunch Moms unless they work. When Cindy Appleton's mom is Lunch Mom, all of the boys in our room begin to finger-comb their hair and wipe up their own crumbs; they pull folding chairs away from the lunch tables without being told 872 times to do so. Mrs. Appleton smiles at the boys as if she likes them, but at the same time she looks like she has forgotten something important, like where she put her car keys or how exactly she got to the point of being a Lunch Mom. When she gets to Cindy Appleton's lunch table, Mrs. Appleton looks like she remembers something very important. Mrs. Appleton dumps the still-full lunch bag contents in front of Cindy Appleton, spreads out the entire food pyramid, and pushes an egg salad sandwich into Cindy Appleton's balled-up fists.

Biology. Sister Quackenpuss sets up the ant farm on the windowsill, and we take turns observing. From far away, it looks like a column of beach sand with handwriting carved into it—like hieroglyphics from Miss Margaret's Egypt lectures—but close up you can see that the handwriting is made of moving ant-ink. *Note their singularity of purpose*, Quackenpuss says. *Ants have one goal— to find food. They follow their leader to the food source; each carries a crumb back to the start.* I can't help but notice the choir-like lift in Quackenpuss' voice. *Try and break them apart; see what happens.* Pauly Harmon pushes a stick into the ant farm, breaks the chain. The new branch starts off in a different direction, but within seconds, loops back to the original chain. *You all have a similar purpose, children.* John Massimo pipes up. *To get to lunch period?* he asks. *To follow the Lord,* New Girl says. How smart she is, I think.

We go to the library for recess when it rains. My mom is a Library Mom (which exempts her from being a Lunch Mom), and she knows better than to call attention to her being my mother when I enter the library, single file behind New Girl. Library Mom/my mom smiles at New Girl. Everyone smiles at New Girl except for Cindy Appleton, who decidedly does *not* smile at New Girl, who in fact, behind her back, whispers *Peg Leg, Hoppy, Cripple* to anyone who will listen to her. The only one who listens to her is John Massimo, and he laughs a pig laugh that makes Miss Margaret turn around and send our row to detention yet again.

We file past the convent and the rectory and the church parking lot and down the hill. It is spring, and so they let us run on the ball field, and it's the boys that run up and down the field, throwing balls at each other and whooping when someone either catches or drops something. At first, it is the boys that run and hop and whoop, but then it is New Girl, too, and it turns out New Girl can not only run and jump like in gym class, but she can field balls, too, and she throws the balls straight and fast to Pauly Harmon, our star pitcher, and then Pauly Harmon grabs New Girl by the hand and he smiles and she smiles, too, and they run, together, behind the ball field, and her hair bounces as they run, and they look so happy that I am not at all worried about New Girl's plastic knee every time her left saddle shoe hits the ground, and they run behind the ball field and behind the bleachers while Cindy Appleton screams at the top range of her soprano—*Peg Leg! Hoppy! Cripple!*

Cindy Appleton has more demerits than Satan. She may not graduate. I would puke, too, if I were Cindy Appleton.

They offer extra credit for things like cleaning up the pews after morning mass and wiping down the blackboards during recess. The same people always go for the extra credit. I always go for extra credit. I am aware that I do not need it, but it keeps me out of the way of the things going on around me that have nothing to do with me. Sometimes when I wipe down the blackboards, I imagine that I only have one leg and that the weight of me is held up by one good leg and one plastic Barbie leg; that my hair is light and bouncy instead of flat with tiny white flakes. I imagine that my plastic leg is actually full of magical powers—that I can run and jump and find a boy to take me down the hill and across the ball field and behind the bleachers.

Pauly Harmon + New Girl = Hot and Heavy. We watch as they fly paper airplanes painted with hearts and loopy daisies back and forth during World Cultures class. No one watches more closely than Cindy Appleton. She is clearly in outer space when Miss Margaret asks her to name the two most important generals of the Civil War. *Abraham Lincoln and George Washington?* Everyone laughs out loud. Pauly Harmon laughs the loudest. Miss Margaret calls Cindy Appleton to the front chalkboard and makes her write out "Robert E. Lee" and "Ulysses S. Grant" a hundred times apiece. Forty-two times in, Cindy Appleton asks Miss Margaret for a bathroom pass.

When they start tacking up Easter eggs and crucifixes on the classroom doors, we know we are in for the dreaded Lent. Forty days of sacrifice. We give up things that are supposed to mean a lot to us. Pauly Harmon gives up pizza. Cindy Appleton gives up lunch (arguably not a

sacrifice). New Girl says she likes a proactive Lent—
she will volunteer once a week at a soup kitchen. New
Girl makes her Lenten declaration and we all nod and
say *Wow*. Even Sister Quackenpuss says *Wow*. This is
a different variety of sacrifice. I consider my options
before declaring my Lenten sacrifice. I was going to
give up chocolate, but now New Girl has made me feel
as stupid as Cindy Appleton. *I like a proactive Lent, too*, I
declare, as loudly as I've ever spoken in class. *I will go to
mass every morning*. I feel proud of my proactive Lent until
I hear John Massimo whisper, *Quackenpuss Junior.*

Miss Margaret must have decided to make an example
out of Cindy Appleton, because each day in World
Cultures, she exploits Cindy Appleton's apparent disdain
for all things world-related. Miss Margaret asks Cindy
Appleton to stand up and answer a question pulled from
the previous day's reading assignment. *Which state first
seceded from the Union? Was Virginia a Union or Confederate
state? Who gave the Gettysburg Address, and please recite the first
line?* Cindy Appleton stands there in the middle of her
aisle and gets question after question wrong, and finally,
after her fifth or so failure, Miss Margaret sends Cindy
Appleton to the board to write out the answers over and
over again. Cindy Appleton's bone structure is poking
out from her uniform at obvious angles. It seems the
more of her weight that disappears, the more visible
she becomes to everyone. *Chicken Legs, Needle Neck, Flatsy*,
John Massimo chants. *Hall pass?* Cindy Appleton asks.

☾

I am usually the only one at morning mass, other than the nuns and old Father Dowd. Father Dowd has a speech impediment, and it is hard to focus on much other than his lispy Jesus'. Morning mass, while representing a proactive Lent, is actually quite passive and—truth be told—dull as hell. I use the forty-day window to perfect the sleep stare. As it turns out, I am quite good at appearing to be engaged while floating around in my mind. Occasionally, it feels as if I'm hovering above my body, watching myself fidget in the pew. Sometimes I do a flyover of Quackenpuss's row, and it looks like she is sleep-staring, too.

Miss Margaret's daily sorties on Cindy Appleton continue from late winter to early spring. *Twiggy, Bones, Barf-o-matic*—John Massimo runs out of nasty-isms and begins to say nothing at all. We have come to expect failure from Cindy Appleton. *Where did Lee's surrender take place?* Cindy Appleton is the color of oatmeal. Her back is toward me, and I can see the sag in her uniform socks. There is a long silence. Pauly Harmon passes a folded note to New Girl, but New Girl ignores him. She too is looking down the aisle, likely staring at Cindy Appleton's legs, their lack of calves. *Appomattox*, New Girl whispers. *Appomattox*, Cindy Appleton says. The entire class applauds; even Miss Margaret applauds. I begin to think that New Girl is like Jesus, only somehow more approachable.

HOW WE LEAVE

The bell rings at 4:30 and we burst through the double
doors of St. Pius X and spill into the schoolyard,
forming queues according to our bus routes. The
individual queues, however, have no rules. They are
not alphabetical; they are not by height. Genders mix,
book bags scatter, kids hopscotch among lines until their
bus shows up at the appointed time. It would be chaos
if it were not for the sixth-grade Safety Squad, whose
members stand at the front of each line with silver-
plated badges in their hands, making sure no one crosses
into the double-yellow school bus lanes. *Click, click, click.*
The Safeties flick their wrists; the silver buckles that hold
the adjustable badges to their hands strike the metal
faceplate and you know they are there, over all of the
shouting and hand-grabbing and line-blending, the
sixth-grade sentinels.

The buses are rarely off schedule, and so we get used
to the order of leaving. Ribbon by ribbon, we realign.
The Safeties step to the side as we board. New Girl's bus
is always first, and so she threads her way from Pauly
Harmon's line back to her own. Her sixth-grade Safety
eye-combs the schoolyard for her. *Click, click, click.* Her
Safety's badge sounds come faster and faster until New
Girl is on the steps of her bus. She looks back over her
shoulder at Pauly Harmon, her smile as broad as Farrah
Fawcett's. Who could deny her this happiness? Legless,
but somehow happy. New Girl's bus drives away and my

attention trails with it. I sleep-stare and begin to drift, in my mind, above everything. I have an aerial view of the schoolyard, and it is beautiful—the wayward scrolls of bodies, the tops of heads forming undefined but industrious colonies. Human forms disappear. Those that are left—Cindy Appleton, Pauly Harmon, John Massimo, and even me, down below—string together, connect, blend into something completely identical.

LUNAR FACTS

1. I am planning to remove the moon from service. Do not consider this a temporary interruption. It will be permanent.

2. Statistics show that over 82 percent of violent crimes occur when the moon is full. Isn't it time we hold the moon accountable?

3. Super moon, blue moon, harvest moon, blood moon a week or so ago that I missed due to major exhaustion from dealing with you, sliver-of-a-moon, Jay Leno's chin moon, eclipsed moon—so much to keep track of, so much sky clutter.

4. We hold hands under a partial lunar eclipse, stretched across the hood of your 4Runner. Your lips sting from sunburn, but we kiss through it. *Aloe tastes like rubber*, you say. The truck hood capillaries cold into my spine. I totally forget to look up at the stupid eclipse.

5. Emergency rooms are an Expandafoam of crazies during a full moon.

6. The moon is so full it is hollow, and now you find yourself busting out words to fill it, words you've never said to me, or—if I believe you—to anyone, ever. You tell me how the moon was full when you woke up in your big-boy crib to the screams of your mother, the slap-sounds much louder than patty-cake slaps punching through the walls of your nursery. You think you tried to crawl out through the bars of your crib; you think maybe your right leg hooked up and under the top rail. You think the sound of you hitting the wide-oak planks of your nursery floor was what stopped your mother's crying, or maybe, you think, the sounds of you crying took over everything—the nursery, the house, the moon, filling up the giant sky circle with the insides of you until its face glowed the color of urine.

7. Experts say that the increased incidence of crimes and erratic behavior on full moon days may be due to "human tidal waves" caused by the gravitational pull of the moon.

8. The last time I took you to the emergency room, there was no moon in the sky whatsoever. I know this because the streetlight in front of your shithole apartment was out again, and it took me forever to find the ignition on your steering column while simultaneously trying to control the tidal wave of you. *A miscalculation*, you said later; *A freak accident*, you said the next time. *You wear me out*, I think, but I do not say.

9. Albert Einstein, when contemplating whether or not properties of particles exist if they cannot be directly observed, stated: *I like to think that the moon is there even if I am not looking at it.*

10. I like to think that you exist even if I am not looking at you. Sometimes, I am not so sure about this, so I open up your medicine cabinet and observe the meniscus of pills in various amber plastic bottles. Quick math. It's like guessing the jelly bean count in the sun tea pitcher at your nephew's birthday party, but I recall being outwitted by an eight-year-old named Brody. I peek around the corner and see you slumped on the futon, mid-Cheetos bag. You exist.

11. Roman historian Pliny the Elder suggested that the brain was the highest water-content organ in the body and therefore the most susceptible to the pernicious influences of the moon, which triggers the tides.

12. Do you remember teaching me to drive stick shift? The almost vacant King of Prussia parking mall garage? Bright-as-hell mercury lamps made it look like noon in there, but it was three in the morning and we stuttered our way up and up the garage ramp and then there was the rooftop and the beach ball of a moon—*Let's drive to Atlantic City*, you said, vodka fumes rising off of your tongue. I distracted you with my combo downshift/hand job. Your whole body was damp to the touch.

13. Lunar fact: Originally, the moon was very close to Earth. Some speculate that there was enough light from the moon to see clearly at night. Which means we would have all lived like summer Alaskans. Which means depression would have become extinct.

14. It is a harvest moon, and your call to me in which you say goodbye sounds like the 724 other times that you've said goodbye to me, except a little more final. You say goodbye and I realize that you haven't even said hello, which is strange, and I say your name, over and over, thinking I hear you breathing on the other end of the phone, but then I'm not so sure. You have not hung up the phone, but you are not there, either.

15. Your therapist said maybe you didn't get enough fresh air. That I should take you outside more. *Try hike therapy*, she said. She had a moon-white lab coat with pockets that she jammed her hands inside of while she talked to me, her fingers wrestling with each other the entire time she gave me the lecture-of-singular-topic—*you*—and I was thinking, *What about me? When does my therapy start?* But of course it never did.

16. I leave your therapist's office and the moon is a tick less than full, and then it is gone, smothered by Fluffernutter clouds. The moon has vanished, but Einstein and I know that it is there.

17. When the moon goes away, when I pluck it from the sky, of course night, as we know it, will be over. The light will be brilliant. You may voluntarily choose to hike. I hope you do. I really do.

DJ'S ADDICTIONS

DJ's addictions always begin in the same place—excitement. DJ is first excited over girls. This we feel is natural. DJ dates the girls and dumps the girls, calendar girls, we call them, because he clicks through them on a monthly cycle. *More like period girls*, DJ says, and at first we laugh because this is funny, talking about menstrual cycles with a sixteen-year-old boy. DJ starts to smoke—blowing smoke rings excites him. Hanging a cigarette out the Altima's window while driving excites him. This is not so funny, but what can we do? We are 50 percent parents. We are, in reality, weekend parents, as—according to the very inexpensive therapist brought in to detraumatize divorce—it is more stable for the children to stay in their own home. DJ's breath smells like smoke, and then it smells like smoke mixed with something else, something pungent, and of course it is Captain Morgan or Johnnie Walker Red, and we say, *DJ, you are grounded*, but of course he is only 50 percent grounded, or maybe 22 percent grounded because he is very slippery and charming and DJ and October switch to odorless Stolichnaya vodka and Altoids, and we begin to breathe again. DJ and November fuck on our couch. DJ and December—who happens to be the fifteen-year-old virgin across the street—fuck under our pool table. *The fucking has to stop*, *DJ*, and we think he is listening, but in case he is not we buy Trojans and put them in his 50 percent nightstand. DJ's breath begins to smell again, and this time it reeks of pot, and we are not—*not*—having this and *This time* we *have to tell your mother*, as if the promise of communication with DJ's mother will stop anything, but of course it does not, and DJ's excitement over pot transcends his excitement over December, who in fact leaves him before the month is out, *before Christmas, for fuck's sake*, and DJ shoots up into January, calendar-girl-less, but he opens a whole new gateway of excitement whose symptoms we can no longer diagnose, and his 50 percent slips to something like 12 percent us and 20 percent his mother and the rest at the house of some kid named Christopher—who is of course nicknamed Topher—and we cruise by Topher's house 100% of the time that DJ is missing, looking for trails of him.

ADOPTING MERCY

It is the seventeenth time when I break. Funny thing is, I wasn't even close the sixteenth time, even though times twelve through fifteen were so close. And after it is over—time seventeen—after we bundle ourselves back together, me all inside out and itchy-seamed, I just want to get the hell home. You drive real slow and ask me if I remember time number one. *Of course I do. I am not stupid.* But my voice gives me away. I was stupid, after all, especially time one when you were sparkly-faced with the classic *Adopt an Orphan* bumper sticker on your forehead. *No!* I'd screamed a jungle-yell in the lobby when you signed me out for the afternoon. You were the first, my first, and it was our first, and it was miserable. Fuddruckers. Choose your meat. I am vegetarian. You looked terrified. *You were*, you said. *I was*, I said. Time two, less crappy, but crappy still. Times three through eight, you introduced me to Frappuccinos and so I knew you were rich. Time nine. *Where's your husband? No husband*, you say. *Dead end*, I think. Time ten I sleep over and your guest room bedsheets feel as soft as cake icing. I dream and I don't like to dream. Time eleven— Ernie. Almost. Blows it. *She likes you*, he says, underfoot like a stray cat. I try to burn him up with my stare, but he pulls my pigtails until I yell, *Mercy*. That's our game,

Ernie and me. Mercy. Figuring out who can hold out in more pain. Thing is, I let Ernie win all the time 'cause I hate to see him do his lose cry. *She likes you*, he says again, releasing my pigtails. I see you smile big, filling up the lobby with your fluorescent teeth, and the thing about it is you look a little like my mom used to look before everything happened. And so, time eleven, I am an asshole. Time twelve—before you show up, I pace the halls and think, no way you are showing. I flash back to time eleven—the Starbucks patio. I kick the iron legs of my chair until everyone looks at us. *Stop!* you say. *You can't tell me what to do*, I say. *You are not my mother. I have a mother. You can never be my mother.* I kick and flap so hard, my Frappuccino burps out of its blowhole. You fast-drive me back to the abandoned kiddie home and we don't even say goodbye. I dream that night, hate that I do, because I see a giant balloon head in a Thanksgiving parade, and it floats up and away into the sides of buildings, and at first the balloon has my mom's face, but as it gets farther away I can see that it is really you. And so, time twelve, Ernie waits in the lobby with me and holds my hand; he doesn't even try to squeeze it off of my arm. *No mercy?* I ask him. *No mercy*, he says. Your Mini Cooper pulls into the visitor spot and I squeeze Ernie's hand until he yelps, *Mercy*.

Times thirteen through sixteen:

13. I meet your parents. Nice but they smell a little like peanut butter, and your mother keeps patting wrinkles out of my clothes.

14. We go to Target and you buy the whole place out. You ask me my favorite color. I say blue—which is my mom's favorite color but I don't tell you that—and you buy a comforter the color of Ernie's eyes, and blue sheets, too, and I want to ask you what this all means but I don't.

15. I sleep over again and you take me to the guest room, except you call it *your room*, and still I don't ask.

16. *How would you feel?* you ask. I want to say *great*, I want to say *awesome*, I want to ask, *Is it a forever thing, because that's what a mother is supposed to be, right?* But I know that, since you're asking, my mother is not a forever thing, that she's a definitely never thing, and so I have no enthusiasm to offer when I answer you. *It'd be OK*, I say. And I can hear you deflate.

17. You are taking me camping. Again, I'm in the lobby, certain I've blown it for real. *So rare to get a match at your age*, they tell me, the ones who watch over us. You drive us up and up a million hills. The Mini Cooper's windows chill and then fog over. We do not say much, until finally, you do. *Do you know why I'm taking you camping?* Your face looks frozen. *No*, I say. *I couldn't face taking you back to my house again*. You stare straight ahead at the road. I stare, too. I'm not sure what's an appropriate adult response here. I am only 12. The silence goes on and on. I want to scream, *Mercy*. End this game. The asphalt in front of us is full of chuckholes. You swerve to avoid the bigger

ones, but we bounce around through smaller dips. This silence is giving me gas pains. *I'll never be your real mother. I know that.* More silence. My real mother—arson, assault, thirty to life. You don't want to be her, I think. I don't want you to be her, either, but I don't say this. I can't say this. *If that's a problem for you, if you can't ....* When you turn to face me, I can see you are crying. I can see snot flowing into the side of your mouth and you choking on the end of your sentence. I can see you need mercy more than me. I put my hand on top of yours on the steering wheel. I squeeze.

GENERAL CONSIDERATIONS OF INDEPENDENT LIVING

As if this day hadn't started crappily enough, waking up to yet another *I can't do this boyfriend thing anymore* text from Gary, I walk into my night shift at Danworthy Independent Living only to find out Mr. Spraker in 78A is dead.

Connie, Danworthy's administrative manager, tells me about Mr. Spraker on her way out the door. "By the way," she says, whipping her car keys around her index finger in a way that looks like she's planning to peel out for a joyride, "you'll need to make the arrangements."

"Make the arrangements? You mean, funeral arrangements?"

Connie laughs. "Jesus, Stephanie, you look pale. Is this your first no-show?"

I must be looking at Connie like my brain's gone pumpkin hollow. She lets go of the front door and heads back behind the counter. "Move over," she says.

"What do you mean, 'no show'?"

Connie grabs the mouse and flicks though computer screens. "A no-show for a meal. You know how old people are—if they miss a meal, they've either fallen and broken a hip or they're taking the 'Big Nap.' Spraker never missed the 5:30 dinner seating. That was the tip-off."

I think about Mr. Spraker, how he always wore a sweater vest, even in August, and how he'd salute me with his rolled-up *Wall Street Journal* every day after his 6 a.m. breakfast.

"Here's the checklist," Connie says, swinging the monitor towards me.

General Considerations upon Death of a Resident.

I scan the list.

Connie points at item one. *Notify Danworthy's director.* "Hal already knows. He said to leave Spraker in place until D'Angelo's can get here." Connie's lifts her keys off the desk. "As if we'd move him. What is this? *Breakfast with Barney?*"

"Huh?"

Connie buttons her sweater so fast it bulges with erratic misalignment. "That movie, you know, the one where they drive the dead guy around for a weekend.?"

"You mean *Weekend at Bernie's?*"

Sometimes Connie doesn't make any sense. I know she's worked at Danworthy for twenty-three years, but it's hard to connect the dots with her. It's like she's lost the perspective that in five or ten years, she could be the one moving in here, and she might want people like me, people like *her*, to have a little compassion. I look down at the lobby desk and see the mess of sudoku and crosswords that Connie's left behind.

"Just follow the checklist. You'll be fine." Connie tosses her permanent wave over her shoulders. "In fact, I can't think of a better person to handle death. You're so sympathetic."

Item two on the *General Considerations upon Death of a Resident* checklist: *Do not discuss the death with any Danworthy resident until the body has been removed from the premises. Maintaining the privacy and dignity of the deceased is of paramount importance.*

I reread Gary's text while I wait for D'Angelo's hearse.

I'm moving out while ur at work. We both know what's really going on. Don't make me say it. I'm the crappiest boyfriend ever. Ur pathetic for taking me back so many times.

Wow. I'm pathetic and sympathetic, all in the same day. I'm about to tweet out one of Gary's dick pics when Mrs. Wobeser from 79A glides up to the front desk. I can't help but smile when I see Mrs. Wobeser—she's decorated her walker in a Hawaiian theme, complete with a fuchsia silk lei and a dashboard hula dancer perched on top of her accessory basket. She seems more with-it than most of Danworthy's residents; in fact, I think she might even get a kick out of Gary's dick pic.

Mrs. Wobeser leans across the counter. "Now tell me what you know about Terry."

"I'm sorry, Mrs. Wobeser, who's Terry?"

"Terry Spraker. 78A, my dear. My next-door neighbor. I thought maybe you'd heard if they found anything …."

Her blue eyes seem to fade a bit and she stares beyond me for a few seconds. This happens a lot with our residents, and I've learned to be patient, wait it out.

"Did they notice anything unusual when they found him?"

Checklist item three. *Determine if the resident has passed under suspicious circumstances. If so, call the authorities and request, on behalf of Danworthy, that an autopsy be performed.*

Mrs. Wobeser's face is unnervingly close; her eyes are back to solid blue and there's a clump of moisturizer stuck to the side of her nose. I'm considering what would be the most thoughtful response to her strange question when two men and a gurney enter the lobby. D'Angelo's.

Mrs. Wobeser knocks on the counter three times—a call to order like the grade school principal she once was. "Let me know what they find," she says. A command.

The problem with Gary is that I've known him since grade school. If I want tacos, he knows to order them on corn tortillas, not flour. He always has a minimum of $17 in his wallet because 17 is his lucky number, and he can make me come, no fuss. Has all of my parts down pat. He's convenient, like so many of these Danworthy "sunset romances," as Connie calls them. *Trapped in here like it's a submarine, what else is there for them to do but screw?* I hate that Connie's put this image in my head, and now I can't help but imagine these old people in a myriad of complicated sexual positions. I found a Kama Sutra app three days ago on Gary's phone—asked him about it since we usually do the same three basic moves, but his face got all cabbage-sour. I downloaded the app after he left, scrolled through page after page of cartoon people—a bright pink man and sun-yellow woman— splayed out on floors, bent over chairs, bat-hanging over a couch or mattress or an exercise ball. Now I'm wondering why I've limited myself; what other ways can I curl and twist?

Once I open Mr. Spraker's front door, the guys from D'Angelo's tell me I can leave if I'd rather not see this. I think about the checklist. I think about Mrs. Wobeser's weird question. I think about the fact that I make $12 an hour, which hardly seems like enough money when this death checklist gives me the authority to order Mr. Spraker split open like a lab rat. I think about Gary, how I'll have to make rent all by myself.

"No, it's OK. I'll stay."

The apartment is quiet, apart from the clicking of the grandfather clock in Mr. Spraker's entryway. The D'Angelo guys walk toward the back of the apartment, but I can't seem to move past the kitchen. This place smells like French toast and pork roll. Yesterday's *Wall Street Journal* is on the counter; the headline: *Domestic Forecast Upswing; GDP Extends Strong Stretch in Q4.* Upswing, yeah, right. A crock of shit for Mr. Spraker and me.

"He's back here."

I want more than anything to run the hell out of here, out of Danworthy, anywhere—even to shithead Gary because if not wanting to see my first dead person is pathetic, then yes, I'm pathetic, but then I flash to Mrs. Wobeser's *tap-tap-tap* on the front counter, recall the steel determination in her eyes—*Did they notice anything unusual?*—so now I'm walking down the hallway, preparing to see blood and smell whatever it is death smells like—some combination of high school biology lab and Gary's laundry basket, I imagine—and instead, I see Mr. Spraker, naked on his bed, spread out corner to corner like a snowflake.

One of the D'Angelo's guys holds up a bottle from Mr. Spraker's nightstand. "Damn—KY Lube! Look at this guy, still going at it."

Checklist item two—preserving dignity—swirls out of my throat. "Put that down." I don't recognize my own voice, the authority behind it.

"Sorry." The guys roll the gurney to the side of the bed. "You OK if we go ahead and move him?"

Checklist item three—suspicious circumstances? I survey the scene. Mr. Spraker's eyes are half-closed; his lips are purpled and parted. Both his arms are outstretched as if, at the very end, he'd been reaching for something.

At the edge of his bed, I see it. One silk fuchsia flower.

By the time this night shift's over and I get home to my empty apartment, I'm dizzy from hunger and stress. I commandeer Gary's side of the bed, wondering if I can sleep him out of my system. Problem is, when I close my eyes, all I see is Mr. Spraker and Mrs. Wobeser flailing their arthritic limbs into positions that seem inadvisable.

Turns out that the Kama Sutra app, which I flipped through with fascination after the D'Angelo crew left with Mr. Spraker, is really more about love than sex—finding a life partner, maintaining an expanding love life, exploring the nature of love. I want to ask Gary if that's what he was trying to do—work on our emotional fulfillment, not figure out how to contort some other girl like a carnival balloon animal—but I know Gary. He likes Xbox games and sex with three-minute foreplay; he's not deep-diving into self-work.

Checklist item four. *Complete the Post-Mortem Incident Report.* The questions on Danworthy's post-mortem incident report keep rolling through me. The only answer I knew by heart was Mr. Spraker's apartment number—78A. The rest, I had to look up in his intake file. Deceased's full name—Terrance Andrew Spraker. Marital status—widower. He was a former wildlife manager for the State of Colorado; he'd been married to his high-school sweetheart, Madeline, for fifty-seven years; she died of cancer right before Mr. Spraker moved into Danworthy. His will was kept on file; he wanted to be cremated and have his ashes spread in the Platte River outside of Golden, Colorado.

Checklists aside, there are so many other things I could have asked Mr. Spraker—why wear a sweater vest in August? Does the early bird really get the worm? Did you ever snowshoe through the Rockies? Live in a yurt? What do you think of Mrs. Wobeser in 79A? Have you ever been to Hawaii? Were the two of you in love?

This is progress—I don't actually want to talk to Gary. I want to talk to Mr. Spraker, ask him all of my

Kama Sutra questions—the ones about the heart, the ones that might make a person sound pathetic: Was Madeline your great love? Did you only sleep with Madeline for fifty-seven years? Was it weird to sleep with someone new after fifty-seven years of Madeline? Would you ever take back a lover, again and again, even if they were a snake? Am I stupid for still thinking about Gary, even a little bit? If I'm asking this question, I'm stupid, right?

Damn, I just let Mr. Spraker walk past me every morning, saluting me with his rolled-up *Wall Street Journal*, never once considering that this man might hold the key to understanding happiness. Just some old dude in a sweater vest. My general consideration was to not consider him in any depth at all. Now, all of Mr. Spraker's wisdom will get dumped into the mighty Platte River.

Maybe I could create a new checklist—*General Considerations of the Living Resident*. All of life's answers are probably right there at Danworthy under one roof, just waiting to be tapped. Maybe I'll start with Mrs. Wobeser—what a gutting thing it was, sitting at her kitchen table telling her the news. She'd made a show of acting as if Mr. Spraker's death was a shock and then asked me again if there was anything odd about Terry's passing. *No, Mrs. Wobeser. He looked peaceful.* It was like lying to Gary all of those times, telling him I could forgive his cheating while my insides filled up with puke. *Well, at least that's something.* Mrs. Wobeser sat up straight as if I'd given her a cue to end our visit. As she righted herself at her Hawaiian-themed walker, I reached into my front pocket, slid the silk fuchsia flower from Mr. Spraker's bedroom floor under a clump of placemats. Why I didn't just throw it in a trash can? Why hide it? I'm sure she'll find the flower one day—things don't ever straighten themselves up on their own. Or maybe they do. Maybe by then, I'll know Mrs. Wobeser's first name.

BOUNTY

Marian's halfway through her beginner Peloton class when she hears her husband, Luke, scream—*What the hell?* She slows her pedaling, listens for his lazy follow-up—*Have you seen my socks? Did you drink all of the almond milk?*—anything that means Marian doesn't have to try and unclip herself from this mechanical beast.

Snails? Are those snails?

Marian twists her ankles outward just like it showed in the Peloton setup video, but she only manages to clip out her right shoe. The left one's stuck.

The screen door slams. *Marian, hurry! You have to see this. There's got to be thousands of snails!*

If they're snails, there's really no hurry, now, is there? Marian grabs onto the red resistance knob in the center of the bike, tries to leverage her ample body weight while twisting her left ankle. Nothing. She grabs her yoga mat, rolls it into a tube, and uses it to pull aside the bedroom curtain. Luke's on the front lawn, bent at the waist like he's pulling weeds. Marian wants to correct the ergonomics of him; in fact, after nine years of marriage, there's much about Luke that she'd like to correct. She reaches for the window latch, yells—*Luke! Your back!*—but her left foot's still a Peloton prisoner. Luke's upright now, swaddling an armful of small, tannish shells. Had it rained last night? Is that where snails come from—the rain? Marian wishes she paid more attention to nature. So much of outdoor life is Luke's department—Boy Scout facts, he calls them— even though Owen hadn't lived long enough for Luke to lead his troop. Owen. He'd loved snails and slugs and tadpoles and all things bug related. He'd play for hours on the lawn with his blue plastic shovel, scooping and pawing, amazed by the simplest grubworm. *He's definitely not your kid*, Luke would tease, back when things were lighter. *You're an indoor cat!* If Owen had been more of an indoor cat—Marian stopped herself. No more what-ifs; isn't that what she'd promised?

It looks to Marian as if Luke's feet are covered in sand. Where's the ryegrass? Now the sand's crawling, a slow tide that's already pulled Luke halfway across the front lawn.

Luke! Marian pitches sideways and hears the click of her left bike shoe as it unsnaps. Her jaw rattles against the windowsill, but she's upright. Outside, Luke's getting swept toward the storm sewer inlet. Marian's gait wobbles due to her bike shoes, so it seems like minutes instead of seconds before she's opening the screen door, leaping onto the front lawn.

Crunch.

Luke's laughing, his arms outstretched. *Marian! Can you believe this?*

The air smells of the sea even though they are dozens of miles from any coastline. Snails cover the bark of the weeping willow tree, mushrooming from every branch and leaf. Snails coat the rhododendron and azaleas and underbrush. Snails smash underfoot as Marian works her way toward Luke.

Head to the street, Luke yells. *It will take them a week to make it there*. He shakes his hands and arms as if they've fallen asleep and he's trying to get his nerves back. Snail shells spray off of him.

When Marian makes it to the street, Luke puts both arms around her, pulls her in tight. He's musky and cold; there's a slimy coating adhered to his T-shirt. Her own tank top and bike shorts wilt with sweat, but still, Marian can't bring herself to tear away.

Did you know snails can see, but they can't hear? Luke asks.

All of these microshells, their tops swirled like perfect cupcakes—none of them processing a single sound, while it seems all that Marian can do right now is hear things—the snap of snails under her bike shoes; that *click click click* of shells, dozens of them, that had hurtled from Luke's arms to the ground; scratches of shells rubbing against the houses of their brothers; the scrape of a tiny plastic shovel.

They're probably destroying our lawn.

Luke loves his lawn. Since Owen, she'd been certain he used yard work as an excuse to drink Bud Lite and get outside—get away from her—but now his voice tins with tears.

Marian considers their lawn as she'd known it, more crabgrass than rye, half-seeded with dandelions. The lawn now, its surface skittering with life. This bounty of snails.

Marian draws closer. She presses her ear into the spot where Luke's clavicle bone indents into flesh; she's certain she can hear Luke's pulse vibrating inside her own cochlea. She wants to ask Luke if he hears Owen sometimes, too, but that might kill this moment for both of them.

Oh, I don't know, Luke. Maybe they're mating.

His heartbeat swells; the way Luke's now pressing into Marian, she senses other swellings, those forgotten possibilities thriving between them.

Do you know how snails mate? Luke lifts Marian up off the ground; she swings into his arms. Shells crackle underfoot, but no one hears them.

GRAVITATIONAL WAVES

Baby Albert reaches through the bars of his crib and grabs the remote control. *Universal remote*, it reads across the top in black letters. This makes him laugh. Baby Albert reaches through the crib bars again, turns off the volume on the Graco monitor. *Why do they feel the need to listen to every breath of mine, every tiny fart?* He settles into a pile of plush toys in the corner of his crib and hits the universal power button. Again, he laughs. *As if the universe could be controlled.* Everything pops on at once—TV, DVR, Bluetooth speakers. The baby sighs. *Same goddamned DVD. Always Baby Einstein—classical music, bunnies, ballerinas.* Disgusted, he drops the universal remote and stares as the crib's mattress seems to bend and mold itself around the spot where the remote first hits and then contracts back as if the ripple had never existed or the mattress hadn't expanded for that fraction of a second. Had he really seen it? Heard it? *Damn it!* If he had left the Graco monitor on, maybe his parents would have heard it, too. Perhaps they would have enough gray matter to understand what it is that he now understands—the fluidity of space, the way it can warp under the influence of gravity.

When his mother walks into the nursery, she is confused. She doesn't remember turning on the DVD.

She doesn't understand how Albert could have gotten hold of the remote, or why he keeps dropping it and picking it back up. Dropping. Picking up. Why he always looks at her as if he thinks she's stupid.

The baby drops the remote one last time and cries out. *She doesn't get it*, he thinks. *I must explain.* He is surprised at his lack of words, his inability to do anything but wail.

THE ERRATIC FLIGHT
PATTERNS OF BATS

The weather is warm again, and the Mexican free-tailed bats have returned from their winter in Jalisco, Sinaloa, and Sonora. They fly overhead. I tilt back in my Adirondack chair, look to see if they etch any trace of you in the sky.

That first night. After the jump.

"Float," you say.

A command. You presume I have control over my body after half a bottle of zinfandel. I focus and quiet my flippery feet, stare at the bug-filled air. Moths and mites skip and hop nonsensically as if they are playing Chinese checkers. I believe I am floating.

"Like this?" I ask.

When you don't answer, I start to sink. But your hands swoop. You gather me.

Mexican free-tailed bats hunt their prey using echolocation. They are primarily insectivores, eating moths, beetles, dragonflies, flies, and wasps—things that they catch in flight.

That first night. Before the jump.

"So I'm a rebound?" you ask.

We sit on the edge of Crumb's pool. It's a pool party in theory, but in practice, no one's in it. I don't know why I've told you about Toby, that other girl, the breakup.

I splash the pool's cool surface with my feet. "Who says you're anything?"

When you laugh, I can see the back of your mouth—a cave. You give the laugh everything that you have and then you jump into the water. You break the surface and smooth your hair with your hands. Water droplets umbrella-drip off of your eyelashes. Even before you hold out your arms, I know that I will jump.

Bat mating can occur in an aggressive or passive form. In the aggressive form, the male controls the female's movements, keeping her away from the other bats in the roost. He also tends to vocalize when mating. During passive copulation, the male flies to a female in her roost and quietly mounts her with no resistance.

(Crumb warns me as I grab my coat. "He's a douche but I love him like a brother." I know Crumb is telling the truth, but I decide to chalk his douche talk up to multiple Bacardi 151 Jell-O shots. My place. You are loud and I am loud and I wonder— have I been doing it wrong all this time?)

Mexican free-tailed bats begin feeding after dusk. This species of bats flies the highest of all species at altitudes around 10,000 feet, and they've been measured at a ground speed of 99 miles per hour.

(You move so fast, you're like a hockey puck that I can't track. I want to track you. I want to fly south with you, then north, then south again—a never-ending zigzag. *I haven't lived yet*, you say, after we hit the six-month mark. *I can't do this boyfriend/girlfriend thing.* Your mouth is still moist with the stickiness of me. *You haven't really lived yet, either.* You think you are helping; you think you are breaking my pattern—jump, attach, stick. You are smug with all of your knowing better, and you move wildly, tripping over my Crate & Barrel throw rug, black underwear balled up in your fingers.)

According to Spanish lore, bats symbolize good health, good fortune, and family unity.

Midnight. The Adirondack chair. Bats fly overhead like crack babies from those anti-drug warning videos—spastic and inconsolable. It is a night like that first night at Crumb's—warm, moonless. My hands are on my belly now, feeling its hardness. A protective shell. I look for patterns in the bats' erratic flight; I know it is pointless, but I have to try.

HOUSE RULES

1969

Samantha and I are both "the babies" when we play house. Samantha has better dolls, so we stage our house in her bedroom. Her closet doors are mirrored, and so when we play house, it's like there are four of us—Samantha, Samantha's twin, me, my twin—and when we skip and dance and laugh, we multiply even more.

1970

The summer heat is brutal. Samantha's house does not have air conditioning, so we play house outside. Samantha's older sister, Lorraine, watches us from a woven lounge chair. She wears a polka-dotted headscarf and sunglasses and reads *Seventeen* magazine. Mostly, she ignores us. When Samantha fake-spills tea over me and my rag doll baby, I scream very realistically, as if my legs are actually burned (they are, but only by the sun). Lorraine looks up, peers at us from over the top of her sunglasses. *Of course, you both play the baby*, she says. Lorraine is only fourteen, but to me she looks as glamorous as Elizabeth Taylor.

1971

Now when we play house, Samantha is the mother and I am the baby. We did not negotiate this. It just happened. Lorraine doesn't sit with us much, even though Samantha's mother tells her she has to. We hear Lorraine yell through the porch door—*You are the mother, not me. Not my fault. You chose this for yourself.* Doors slam inside the house. Samantha picks up the aluminum pan from her Easy-Bake Oven and wallops my buttocks. *Bad baby. Bad.*

1972

Samantha's mother had to get a day job on account of Samantha's father leaving. We play house at my house. I am still the baby every time. The dolls we use as my siblings are split at their seams. My mom allows us to wander the neighborhood as long as we come back when she rings the cowbell. Sometimes, we sneak all the way up the steep hill to Samantha's house, our mission: to spy and catch Lorraine doing something she shouldn't be doing so that Samantha can rat her out. One time, we see Lorraine smoking a cigarette on the back patio. *Ut-oh,* I say. *She's in big trouble.* But Samantha says no, her mother knows all about it. I think they play house differently up here than we do down there.

1973

I drag my new doll, Velvet, up the hill, excited to show Samantha how Velvet's hair can be long or short, just by turning a knob on her back. Samantha does not want to play house. *House is for babies. I am not a baby*, Samantha says. Her voice sounds like a soap opera star, a little like Lorraine's.

Michele Finn Johnson

1974

Lorraine is gone. No one will say where she went. Samantha says she doesn't know. Samantha also says she doesn't want to play anything anymore. Samantha stays in that dark house, up the hill, all summer. Sometimes I climb up the hill and try to peek through her windows, but all of the rooms are dark. I go home, pull ragtag dolls out of my closet and have a tea party. My closet door does not have a mirror, like Samantha's, and so we are alone.

THE CIRCUMFERENCE
OF EVERYTHING

It's Cory's idea to drive a Vanagon around Iceland to save his marriage. He couldn't have known that the rental agency only had stick shift Vanagons, that Natalie—the only standard transmission driver between them—would have to be the one to drive the entire circumference of Iceland.

"Iceland? More like wholly barren Crapland," Natalie says.

Cory cringes. He navigates Natalie past pungent mudlands to Reykjavík's famous hot springs, hopeful for their claims of restorative powers. Restoration—isn't that what all marriages need after a decade?

Cory delights in the vision of Natalie entering Reykjavík's pool, pleased she's chosen to be naked. Her belly is deflated. Steam catches inside her curls, freezes into a thousand icicles.

For a moment, Cory feels everything—heat, vapors, the soft rub of Natalie's elbow against his, the stony quiet of their loss—then, finally, peace.

It's the too-rapid flush of Natalie's skin that drives them out of the pool and back into the Vanagon.

"I can't feel the freakin' wheel," Natalie says, waving purpled hands. "You're going to have to shift."

And so they make their way along Iceland's circumference like that—Natalie clutching, Cory steering and shifting, the occasional misfire and correction, the tiniest breath of frost between them.

FRAT PARTY

1. Lie on twin-sized bunk bed and think about whether or not it's smart to go to Delta Sig. You wonder where your roommate is; you think you saw her on Wednesday but you really can't be sure.

2. The number of empty hangers in your three-by-five-foot dorm closet far exceeds the number of hangers with clothes still on them.

3. The goldfish tank is your roommates'. Kim and Kanye swim in and out of the glitter castle, unaware of their missing owner. You shake fish food flakes onto the top surface while you think about Grant Davenport—his rugby legs, sexy-scruff face, his *You should drop by tonight*. Before you know it, your dorm room smells like crab; Kim and Kanye bloat with excess.

4. Back to your bunk. How many people have slept on this bed? How many people have done it on this bed? Why haven't you done it on anyone's bed? Could you do it on Grant Davenport's bed? Whose bed is your roommate doing it on right now?

5. The pile of dirty clothes at the bottom of your three-by-five-foot closet cannot be totally tamed with Febreze,

but your Lucky jeans seem significantly improved. You put on a sequined tank top (roommates'?) and deem yourself half ready.

6. Kanye stares at Kim and they mouth to each other in slow-motion bubbles. It looks totally romantic until you see that Kanye is excreting a long, black thread.

7. There is a hole the size of a fist in Delta Sig's front door.

8. Song on blast is Kanye West, and you find that hysterical. *I seen you before, but don't know where I seen ya. Oh I remember now, it's something that I dreamed of.* White boy frat house trying to be hip-hop cool. Maybe channel that cool while you stand, alone, in the doorway of Delta Sig. Maybe chill when you see Grant Davenport at the pool table, aiming for the purple four ball. Maybe try not to wobble on your high-heeled Toms when he smiles at you.

9. In the Delta Sig hammock with Grant Davenport after two healthy dips of trash can punch. His scruff burns across your face when you make out. Somehow, the palm of his hand has made it up and under your sequined top, your bra, your Lucky zipper. When he touches your panties, he calls you Marsha. It's close, but this is not your name.

10. Maybe your roommate is dead in a shallow grave; maybe her three-week boyfriend has her duct-taped

in his three-by-five-foot closet; maybe your roommate is on some kind of medication and, without it, she forgets that she is, in fact, your roommate. Maybe your roommate needs you. Maybe your roommate needs you *right now!*

11. Kanye again. *Get your mind right baby or get your shit together*.

12. Your high-heeled Toms tangle in the hammock's webbing; Grant Davenport shouts *Shit, Marsha*, as you right yourself, swim back through Delta Sig, back up where you began.

SAFETY

Heidi Sutherton disappeared from Lumitown in the summer of 1973. She was seventeen years old—seven years older than my best friend Margaret and me—and lived right across the street. Our next-door neighbor told us the news—Mrs. Carmichael, with her chin mole shaped like a pencil eraser. *Snatched right in front of the house*, Mrs. Carmichael told my mom. Margaret and I eavesdropped while we played Maui Beach under the weeping willow, arranging Beach Barbie and Malibu Ken side by side on Burger King napkin beach blankets, their plastic hands and legs mashing in a way that seemed illicit. *On her way to Bible Study. The shame of it.* There was something about their huddled adult heads, the buzz of the word "shame," that made Margaret and me look up. Mrs. Carmichael pointed at us. *I'd keep those girls inside. That's what I'd do if I had a girl in this town.*

Lumitown's night sky was filled with Batman beams from search copters; cones of light shone down on forests of blue spruce and wild holly. Our town sounded like the nightly news reports from Vietnam, the Hueys and their deafening pulses of air. I stared out my bedroom window at the strange light show, looked beyond it to Heidi Sutherton's house. Shadows moved behind Heidi's bedroom curtains. I imagined police officers, search dogs. Maybe they were reading Heidi's diary for clues. It wouldn't take much for them to figure out about that boy Conrad—the one who crept into the Sutherton's yard at night and threw rocks at Heidi's window until she'd appear in her sunflower nightgown and wave him off. Heidi told me about Conrad one time that she babysat me while she French-braided my hair.

There's this boy who likes to brush my hair, she'd said. *His name is Conrad. He tells me I'm magic.*

Magic? Like the Ouija board you showed us?

Heidi threaded three bunches of my hair through her fingers, tightened her grip as she wove my braid. *Kind of like that, Lucy, but not quite.*

I liked the feel of Heidi's fingers manipulating my thin scraps of hair into a pattern, her smell of patchouli and cool breath on the back of my neck. *Is he your boyfriend?*

Heidi laughed. *Oh Lucy, if it were that simple.* She gave my braid a tug. *Conrad's not like us. He's different—too different.*

I had visions of Sesame Street, how frogs could date pigs. *But different is good, right?*

Heidi reached the bottom of my braid. *Remember how Ouija was our secret?* She wrapped the ponytail with an orange-beaded tie. *Conrad is a secret, too.*

After that day, I tried to keep watch over Heidi, running to my bedroom window if I heard rock sounds at night. I thought I saw the dark shadow of Conrad at least twice, Heidi's hands waving goodbye to him and then the scratch of her window shutting. Ever since she went missing, Heidi's bedroom light glowed honey yellow all night long. I wondered if she'd still want me to keep her secret.

There was no trace of Heidi. Margaret and I were forbidden to walk the half block to each other's houses or to go outside alone. *Can't I just play in the backyard?* Mom slapped her hands on her apron. *What kind of mother would that make me?* Mom looked as frenzied as Heidi's mother did on Eyewitness News. Heidi's story was on TV every night, even before the Vietnam updates and the photographs of all the lost boys.

The doorbell rang and it was Margaret, alone. I looked past her, up and down the tree-lined street. *How did you get here?*

Margaret looked at me like I had my finger up my nose. *I escaped*, she said. She skipped her way past me to my backdoor. *We can't leave Barbie and Ken in Maui forever to rot, now can we?*

Truth is, I'd forgotten about Barbie and Ken, the beachfront paradise we'd carved out for them in the flat spots between the weeping willow's roots. We abandoned them the day Heidi disappeared. I didn't look back that day to see if Mrs. Carmichael watched us go inside, but I know she did. That summer after Heidi disappeared, Mrs. Carmichael kept guard over Margaret and me from behind darkened curtains, yelling if either of us let out a play scream—*You girls OK?* Mrs. Carmichael protected us in ways we couldn't see but could only feel—like the glassy pull of a Ouija planchette, the same pull that told Margaret and me, later that summer, that Heidi Sutherton was dead, long before they found her remains under sticks and rotted leaves in Ridley Park. The same slick pull that slid the planchette past YES, past NO, when we called upon Heidi Sutherton, asked her if she was safe—the open circle hovering over GOODBYE.

THE ART OF A COVENANT

*"Supreme excellence consists of breaking the enemy's resistance
without fighting."*
—Sun Tzu, *The Art of War*

Jon trudged through snow-covered Philadelphia
streets, wondering if Carla would say yes this time to his
third and—he swore—final proposal. It was the first real
snow of the season, over three inches had fallen in three
hours, and Jon wasn't prepared for the wet walk, his
Florsheim shoes slick and porous. The snowfall brought
an unusual stillness to the city, and it was the lack of
sound that seemed to amplify Jon's inner thoughts.
Carla. The thought of marrying her made Jon's frozen
feet thaw a bit—her Rapunzel hair, the way her clothes
smelled like lemons, how she'd avert her eyes from him
while they ate, never telling him to close his mouth when
he chewed. Jon paused at each intersection, watched as
cars and SUVs and buses slid through red lights and
stop signs. At every pause, Jon poked a mitten into his
coat pocket, feeling around for the tiny white box. Still
there. Jon had prepared himself for this, his third and
final attempt at winning Carla, by immersing himself
in the self-help section at Barnes & Noble. He'd found
solace in Sun Tzu's *The Art of War. When you move, fall*

like a thunderbolt. He crossed Pierce Street and saw the orangey glow of Carla's porch light.

Carla answered the front door, surprised to see Jon's Peking-duck-shaped bald spot through her peephole. When she opened the door, she saw him on one bended knee, a tiny square box in his mittened hands. "Aaaaagh," Carla screamed, a scream like you'd hear in a *Dateline* murder reenactment. The doorknob froze to her hand. She slammed the door shut.

Later that night, she'd supposed that she should have seen this coming. Jon wasn't like the others before him, the ones who gave up at any one of Carla's hundred fake reasons to break up. She called this her fuck-off list, most notably successful so far: *You smell like maple syrup*; *You eat peas one at a time*; *You clump the sugar bowl with your wet coffee spoon*. In fact, Jon had never asked for a reason why Carla rejected each of his two prior proposals. This, Carla realized, was really weird. "Should we order in some aloo gobi?" Jon had asked, immediately after she'd rejected the first proposal. Carla had looked for a hit of sadness in Jon, but there'd been nothing. "Sure," she'd said, knowing that when Jon ate all of the potatoes out of the aloo gobi, she wouldn't say a word about it. They ate take-out Indian food on Carla's sectional couch while watching a *Die Hard* movie marathon on TBS. The second proposal had been more of a production. Flavor of India Restaurant. Dine in. Diamond ring in the parfait glass of rice pudding. Jon had simply wiped the ring clean in his saffron-colored napkin, slid it back into his pocket, and proceeded to eat the rice pudding with his signature open-mouthed chew.

After Carla slammed the front door in his face, Jon stood up and knocked quick three taps, their secret, syllabic code for "I love you."

Carla knew he was expecting her to rap back in four slower taps—"I love you, too"—but she couldn't make her hand do it. Her fuck-off list flooded into her mind all at once—*Your toenails click when you walk*; *You call a library 'li-berry'*; *You wear socks with sandals*. But that was just it—in her entire litany of fuck-offs, none applied to Jon. None. She started to wonder what would it mean to actually go through with it—to marry Jon.

Jon rapped on the front door again—*taptaptap*. I love you.

Bile formed in the back of Carla's throat. She knew she couldn't say no again and get away with take-out tikka masala and *Live Free or Die Hard*. She clenched her hand in front of the door—she air-rapped a *taptaptaptap*, unable to connect.

"Carla, love, I can hear you in there."

Carla had always been exceptional in a crisis—clearheaded, able to see fact and separate it from hysteria, like the night her father hanged himself in their attic. It was Carla, not her incoherent mother, who'd talked to the police. She'd showed them her father's medicine cabinet. Walter's Walgreens, he'd called it, full of pills the color of Carla's favorite spices—cinnamon, turmeric, fenugreek. Curry ingredients, she now realized, as she stared at the only thing standing between her and another disaster. She would need a new type of fuck-off catalog. Something irrefutable.

"Jon, I'm joining the convent."

Jon put his hand on the doorknob.

Seize something that your opponent holds dear; then they will be amenable to your will.

At first he thought he'd heard Carla's breath through the door—thick, more like panting—and then he was sure he'd heard her voice, the way it cracked when she rooted for Bruce Willis to save his movie wife, Holly; Carla's inner optimism revealed.

Betting equals belief. Bet on yourself, Jon.

The doorknob gave way too easily. Jon's Florsheims glided like toboggans on Carla's marble floors, and then there they were, standing eye to eye.

"Carla, I'm marrying you." It was out of him so fast, he hadn't realized that he hadn't actually asked Carla to marry him. He'd told her he was marrying her. *Never venture, never win!* Jon felt like Bruce Willis at the end of *Die Hard*, unstrapping Holly's watch and watching as the bad guy fell down the face of the New York City high-rise.

"Jon, didn't you hear what I said?" Carla felt her voice breaking. "I'm joining the convent!"

Fill silence with silence.

It was as obvious as night that Carla was scared. Jon held his breath and waited for a glimpse of the Carla that rooted for the hero to save the girl. The Carla who wanted a guarantee.

To Carla, Jon seemed altogether different that night. Strong. Declarative. Prepared. It was she who seemed to have a wobble in her knees. Her mind was ablaze with a new Roman Catholic vocabulary of fuck-offs. Each one she squeaked to Jon seemed weaker than the next. "I want to be a nun, I've been called by God to serve, I've always known."

Jon didn't blink.

You can be sure of succeeding in your attacks if you only attack places that are undefended.

"I love you, Carla. I am going to marry you. I am going to protect you."

Carla let out a final chirp "Jon, I'm gay."

Jon grabbed Carla's left hand with his mittened left, and even through a thick layer of wool he could feel it—the break before the actual break. The chalky pallor of her face. Tremors. The same look she'd get whenever she saw prescription bottles in his medicine cabinet. "I have high cholesterol," he'd try to explain, but Carla would always storm away.

Jon squeezed Carla's hand.

Appear weak when you are strong and strong when you are weak.

He dropped to one knee.

Carla looked down. All she could see was the gleam of snowflakes-turned-shiny water droplets in Jon's comb-overed hair. Like diamonds, she thought. Jon's owl stare pierced her and she let out a long sigh, releasing a lifetime of nits and picks and fuck-offs and no-no-no's. Jon was not the same. She could choose to not be the same, too. She watched as a tiny white box tumbled out of his hand onto the marble floor.

Carla closed her eyes while Jon retrieved the fumbled box. "But why, Jon? Why on Earth would you want to marry me? I'm a mess."

Be extremely mysterious, even to the point of soundlessness.

Jon waited for Carla to open her eyes. When she did, Jon flipped open the lid to the little white box. He said nothing. The diamond was brilliant. Emerald cut. The orange glow from Carla's porch light refracted through the stone, casting cinnamon rays onto Carla's living room walls.

Carla dropped down to her knees, nose to runny nose with Jon. "Why, Jon?"

To subdue the enemy without fighting is the acme of skill.

Jon slipped the ring onto Carla's finger. He let go of her hand long enough to knock on the marble floor three times—*taptaptap*. When he heard four slow taps return to him off of the marble, he thought they sounded like horse claps—tiny warriors returning, victorious, from a thousand battles.

RETURNING TO KARAKONG

It was an earthquake—Ida knew at least that much.
Pots and pans flew overhead. Her beloved cat, Squeak,
scampered at her feet; his claws pierced the hem of her
housecoat. Another tremor. Ida swung around, grabbed
for the kitchen counter. Ball-and-chain Squeak slowed
her momentum, tilted her off course. Ida lingered over
the details afforded by each millisecond of the fall—the
grease slick of her counter (damned breakfast bacon);
the pointy edge of her kitchen table; black scuff marks
from her orthopedic shoes on the linoleum floor (she
really should have hired Merry Maids years ago); shards
of her china teacup collection splayed around her like
a sharp, floral rain; Squeak's open-eyed plea—*Don't fall
on top of me!*; the tear of hip muscle away from bone—a
relief, Ida thought, those tight hips, it's time something
gave way, so arthritic; oh, how her mattress pierced her
hips like a hunk of solid granite—and then she was
there, Karakong Rock at Cobbs Creek, the sacred spot
where her father took her as a child; the rock the size of
a small cutter ship jutting out over the water, moss and
granite absorbing the sun's heat; Ida is wearing a white
eyelet shirt and coral pedal pushers; she lays down on
Karakong Rock; its surface curves to meet her body; it
warms Ida from the outside in.

PLAN B

It's not like I don't know what Trent and I are in for. We're both still single, both back in Philly, both drunk on multiple two-for-ones. My heels are inappropriately high for Kelly's Taproom, and I wobble as we walk out the back door. Trent grabs my arm to steady me; I lean into him more than necessary. Purposeful seduction. Trent's weakness is sex and my weakness is Trent, and this seems to have gotten us, intermittently, from college to where we are today—in the parking lot of Kelly's, surrounded by the smoke of overcooked potatoes and the orangey glow of Lancaster Avenue. We lean on the passenger door of Trent's Ford Escape.

Come over here, Trent says.

Our kissing is familiar, even though it's been five years and two failed engagements (mine). He tastes faintly of cucumber and cherry, the girly drink I'd teased him about ordering—*What would the Villanova rugby team think?* I'd asked, but Trent had just lifted up his glass, extended a pinky while he gulped.

We break. I feel the scruff burn from Trent's eleven-o'clock shadow rise on my upper lip.

We could have ... Trent mumbles. He's walking away from me to the driver's side of the Escape, his hands buffalo-stomping in his pockets.

I'm not sure what I'm seeing. I wipe my tongue across my front teeth, park it there like I used to do in college during calculus exams.

Trent finds his keys, beeps his car locks. They click open.

We could have what?

Trent's head hangs limp. Clumps of hair fall over his face, the velvety mass of a closing theater curtain. *Nothing*, he says.

Trent. My sure thing. That kiss was grand. I'd felt the way he'd pushed into me; I can still feel the ghost of it on my thigh. There's a ginny haze that's derailing my common sense to leave this whole question mark alone, and, at the same time, clarity. Occam's razor. The simplest answer.

Who is she?

Trent's face lifts up; he stares at me the same way he did that night in Falvey Library when, while studying for midterms, the fog of differential equations had lifted off of me and—oh so abruptly—I could completely understand the Power Rule, deftly apply the Chain Rule; I was the female equivalent of Sir Isaac Newton—a bemused Trent had just stared while I correctly approximated the distance between points A and B, determined the limit of all of the sequences in our problem set as they approached infinity, as they approached X, as they approached null value.

WATCHING THE CRASH
IN SLOW MOTION

Momma sets me on her lap and tells me my boy-friend's in a coma.

What's a comma?

She plays with my hair like she does when she reads me bedtime stories. *It's called a coma, Mandy, not a comma. It's like sleeping, but more like when you have a cold and your head feels funny and you stay in bed all day.*

She makes it sound like he's just taking a long nap and that we'll be back to sharing PB&Js and riding our bikes together real soon. But a whole week's gone by and still, no boyfriend.

What's he in again?

C-O-M-A.

She spells it for me so that I can get it right when I bring my boyfriend's helmet in for show and tell. It's a big deal, his helmet. I keep hearing Momma on the phone with the other mommas—*If only he'd worn a helmet; If only Mandy had been there—she would have made him wear his helmet; If only helmets were permanently attached to our kids' heads.*

She's wrong. My boyfriend hates his helmet, says wearing it is like having his head crammed inside the jaws of a snake. He stuck his helmet inside my Little

Baker's oven a while ago, asked me to make him some brownies in it. He's funny, my boyfriend. He talks like a cartoon, which is why I let him be my boyfriend. Danny Massimo used to be my boyfriend, but then he picked his nose and wiped it on me. Last show and tell, Danny Massimo brought in his pet hamster. Danny tapped and tapped on the side of the terrarium, but his hamster didn't move one bit. My boyfriend's helmet will be way better in show-and-tell than that dumb hamster. I'm going to wear my boyfriend's helmet and tell my class that Danny Massimo's stupid hamster was in a C-O-M-A. I wish my boyfriend could be there to see it. Maybe he'll wake up in time. If not, I'll imagine him there on his rollout mat, hugging his knees, whistling like Thomas the Train when he sees it's his helmet I'm wearing on my head. *Where are my brownies?* he'll ask, and I'll tell him, *You can't eat brownies in your sleep, Silly! You need to wake up!*

BORN AGAIN

Stephen is a member of the PraiseTheLord club—he has their bumper sticker on his Grand Prix—and so I know that he is off-limits. Untouchable or, at best, touchable above the belt. But that's just it—I want to touch him. More specifically, I want to lick his cherry lips—lick them until they fuzz over with chap and fall off. He doesn't suspect this of me, the girl he *just so happens to bump into* in the apartment complex laundry room every Wednesday night. I think it might send him into evangelical convulsions.

"You're pathetic," my roommate Janet says, watching me pull clean clothes off of hangers, top off two laundry baskets with Downey-fresh shirts.

I drop the baskets in our hallway and do a headstand against the wall. "I know I am. But at least you're getting your laundry done for you."

"You're roommate of the year, Lucy, but you're also kind of freaky."

Janet doesn't really get me. She's got a long-distance boyfriend, Henri, spelled with an "I" because he's super-French, complete with the accent and an addiction to *champignons*. I happen to think Henri's Frenchness makes him less attractive, more Manhattan asshole, but Janet loves it, soaks it up like a syrupy waffle.

"Why in the world do you stand on your head?"

I don't answer Janet until I feel my feet start to numb up and my head get tingly. "It's inversion therapy. Seriously? You've never tried it?" I flip down off the wall, steady myself while blood surges out of my head like thermometer mercury. "It's a yoga move, Janet. Promotes clear thinking."

Janet laughs. "If only," she says. "Maybe then you'd give up your fake boyfriend."

☾

When I get to the laundry room, I can see I'm a tad too late. Stephen's gone already; his jeans/towel load is busy agitating. I invert and do a headstand right in front of the washing machine, watch the endless frothing of Tide bubbles. Stephen's zippers and pant legs and washcloths dart up against the convex window. I think about the time I emptied the dryer for him, found a crumbled business card in the lint catcher—*Stephen Gordon, Engineer*. Maybe Janet's right. Maybe I am losing it, stalking an evangelist engineer in a humid, hot, cramped laundry room. The thing is, Stephen is perfect—electric-white teeth, the smell of Listerine on his breath, hair the color of the fake lump of coal they sell at Spencer's at Christmastime. Stephen is my future; I just know it. But still, staring at his spin cycle, I can't but help to think that I've lost my beans. All for a guy who's never even asked me my name.

The laundry room door opens after untold minutes into my headstand.

"I'm sorry, am I holding you up?"

It's Stephen. Funny, looking at him upside-down, I can see that his sneakers are scuffed red with Carolina clay and his track pants are about an inch too short, likely overdried on the high heat setting instead of permanent press. When I descend from my inversion and turn right side up, Stephen's head looks kind of fuzzy to me, like I'm staring at him through cheesecloth. And then, everything fades to black.

☾

When I wake up, bright sodium lights hover above me. I'm in a hospital room, and I must be pumped full of something because I feel as if I'm suspended in a hammock. I can't read the big "E" on the eye chart on the wall, even though I know it's an "E." Everyone knows it's an "E."

"You're awake."

I look over to the voice; it's Stephen. "Hi, Spin Cycle," I say.

"Hi, Lucy." Stephen walks over to me and grabs my hand, clamshells it in between his.

He is real. His hands are warm, like towels fresh out of the dryer.

"You know my name?"

Stephen smiles, all fluoride and Colgate poster boy-like. "Of course I do."

When I think about this later, I'll realize that I was wearing my tennis team polo shirt that night in the laundry room, the one that has loopy, purple embroidery that spells out my name on the front pocket. But Stephen, ever the Southern gentleman, will not tell me this. He will tell me, instead, about how he, too, loves to do headstands. How it stimulates endorphins, makes him feel alive. Reborn. How it reminds him of his childhood in Savannah, of monkey bars; how he never would let go of the bar until he saw stars. How he wonders if that's what I saw, before I blacked out—a Milky Way of stars. How he wonders if I will be OK once I am upright. How he wonders who, exactly, I am.

BREAKING THE CHAINS

When I call you on my allotted Friday, your answer to my opening question is always the same—*Crazy busy*.

I close my eyes when you answer the phone. In my head, we are nineteen and in my dorm room bed. You're halfway through a bowl of Orville Redenbacher—your hands are buttery and when you reach for my TV remote, I lunge away. Your blanket drops. You are striking in your Dokken T-shirt. The double Ks are thunderbolts, and your hair looks like woven chains.

I give myself orders to keep busy until next Friday's call: Throw away take-out clamshells, shred old bank statements, wipe out the crumbs from the silverware drawer, look for expired cans of non-perishables in the pantry. That's the kind of oxymoron you'd find funny—expired non-perishables—and so I grab the phone to call you, even though it's Wednesday and you've been very clear that my day to call is Friday.

Crazy busy. I hear Wolfgang barking in the background. Someone yells, *Apple juice!* Your telephone rattles to a stop on your countertop. The vacuum seal of your fridge breaks open; kiddos squeal. Wolfgang pants his fuzzy tongue directly into the receiver.

Are you mad at me? It's Friday and you're not answering the phone. I know I shouldn't, but I'm doing this—I sniff my dress khakis (you would say *Gross!*) and search for an unwrinkled polo shirt, one without an IT company logo, but I don't have any of those. I get in my Camry, turn on the AM radio, and scan for news about ten-car pile-ups or local house fires (*Ha! Who's the dramatic one now?*). When I pull up to your curb (*Is that too close?*), your min-ivan's in the driveway (*BTW, the nineteen-year-old version of you would hate the twenty-nine-year-old version of you*). I drive straight home and hit redial.

He answers the phone. *She's busy*, he says. *I know*, I say—*crazy busy*. He pauses. *This is stupid, you calling to talk to a dog*. It sounds like he has some of Wolfgang's fur in his throat. *We can't expect you to understand*, I say. I like invoking the word "we" as if it is "you and I" that are primary and "he" is other, "he" is odd-one-out, the one who missed the best version of you—kohl-circled eyes with a heavy-metal soundtrack; the way you'd throw your head back and swallow cheap tequila with no hands, pull me out on the dance floor and solo air-guitar to Dokken or Ratt; the cool chick, the one who taught me how to touch a girl and be with a girl and buy a dog with a girl and get left by a girl and go nuts over a girl. I'm so whipped up about 1984 you, I forget he's still on the phone. *I'll go get Wolfgang*, he says, like a ding-dong.

It almost kills me, but I wait three Fridays before I call you again. *Take him*, you say. I do not expect this. *Wolfgang,*

that's what you want, right? What you've always wanted?
Something is missing in your voice; I can tell there's no
crazy, no busy left inside of you. I listen for the sounds of
your life—babies, the ice dispenser, microwave popcorn,
the washing machine agitator, an unbalanced ceiling
fan, Wolfgang, even Ding-Dong—but it's silent. It's just
us. *You still there?* you ask. Your voice is powdery; maybe
you've just woken up from a nap. I want to speak, but
now all I can see are your braids on my pillow, those
Dokken tee thunderbolts. There's a family of dead bees
lying next to me on my windowsill; they've been there
for at least a month but I don't have the heart to sweep
them away. I want to tell you about them—I know you'll
understand how sad it all is, but now you are up and
moving. You leave our line open and go on about your
business. Cabinet doors creak open. Hamburger Helper
rattles in the void space of a cardboard box. Cabinet
doors bang shut. Somewhere far away from you and me,
Wolfgang barks and barks. You slide a screen door open
and yell, *Wolfgang! Quiet!* Wolfgang goes silent. Kiddos
squeal. Another Friday night begins.

JERICHO FALLS

They all die the same way in our town. We've come to expect the dying in Jericho Falls, so when it happens—Mrs. Ramirez, the high school chemistry teacher, Bea from Bea's Sweet Shop, or even beloved Father Salazar—we don't cry so much as nod. We all know things about the factory and its big, black smoke belches. Some say that we should do what the people in that old mining town in central Pennsylvania did— abandon ship. Those folks didn't have a choice, probably, what with the ground giving way underneath their houses and streets. That town swallowed its people while they slept. Our town is a little sneakier than that. It coats you—a fine layer of poison dust, thinner than a communion wafer, lighter than the Holy Ghost himself and just as much a mystery. The EPA people say *It's fine*; *it's safe*, but notice they don't live here. Notice they don't stay late enough to witness that smokestack turn from cloud-white to crud, or come early enough to watch us hose off our cars in the morning, dark flakes running into the gutters. When we burn that factory down, we will leave a pile of rubble and cinders stacked so high, even Google Earth will notice it. If you zoom in enough, you might be able to see the dots of our heads, witness us scrambling up, over, out.

THREE IS A RATIONAL NUMBER

Lola's lost her rational numbers worksheet. She's got the whole school bus looking for it—when Lola says to do something, it's like she's an orchestra conductor and we all just fall in line.

"For God's sake, people, it was here a second ago. Look a little harder." Lola's golden ponytail flops side to side as she paces the aisle. She taps Billy Maguire on the top of his head. "What? You give up already?"

Billy Maguire is the goon of Darby Junior High. He's easily a head taller than me. I stand up and start toward them; sometimes it's no fun being Lola's twin brother. My stomach's cramping into a raisin, but then I see Maguire rip a sheet out of his spiral notebook.

"I copied mine for you," he says.

Lola combs over Maguire's sheet as if she's grading it or might even reject it. I'm certain her original homework was wrong because she copied off of mine and I'm an algebraic head case. Billy Maguire's a goon, but Billy Maguire is also the smartest kid in the seventh grade. That's how I know life isn't fair. Lola folds Maguire's offering into her training bra and plops down next to him. I taste this morning's Cheerios backing up in my throat.

Typical day now. Lola and Maguire are holding hands at the bus stop. It's 7:45 a.m., which makes it even grosser.

My best friend, Seegs, is obsessed with two things—*Soldier of Fortune 3* and sex. He points at Lola and Maguire. "How far do you think they've gone?"

I think about decking Seegs, but he's a compulsive nosebleeder. It's messy, and a weird part of him loves the taste of blood. "That's my sister, you perv."

Everything I know about sex I've learned from Seegs. He knows practically nothing, but his brother told him stuff and he's at State College. It's sick to think about Maguire, his monster lips and hands oozing over my sister. Or maybe more. From the pictures Seegs showed me, the whole thing looks pretty impossible. Like winning a game of *Soldier of Fortune 3* against Seegs.

"Yeah," Seegs says. "But do you think he's gotten into her bra?"

According to Seegs' brother, once you get under the girl's bra, you're home free. I tried to talk to Lola about it the other night; I asked her if Maguire was behaving himself, which sounded cornball the second I said it. Lola gave me an eye roll, the one she usually gives Mom or Dad when they turn off a PG-13 movie because it's "too risqué." I don't blame her. I sounded like a freaking Pilgrim.

The school bus pulls up, and Lola and Maguire are the first to climb in. They prefer the first bench, the one everyone has to pass when they board. Maguire's cronies slap him a high five as they walk by. Lola glows with her new secrets.

It's official—I'm rocking a solid C-minus in algebra. Lola is pulling straight A's, and Mom looks mystified as she posts Lola's successes on the front of our fridge.

I elbow Lola as she reaches for the milk. "Those are Maguire's A's, you know."

"Try and keep up," she says. The way she laughs reminds me of Maguire and his friends, their roars that pierce all of us outcast gamers.

After dinner, we sit at the kitchen table and do our homework like we have since we were six. Lola leaves after half an hour, and when I look at her algebra papers, I can see she's barely touched them. Why does algebra matter so much—does it really develop real-world problem-solving skills? Lola seems to be solving all sorts of things by herself without even touching this stuff.

Two months later. Lola bolts to the back of the bus, waving at Seegs and me.

"Let me in," she yells.

She oreos herself in between us and grabs both of our hands. She's pale, like the time our family went snorkeling and a school of stingrays circled around her.

Maguire marches back to us.

"I guess she doesn't want you that bad," one of his goonies yells.

Lola squeezes my hand hard. "He made me touch it," she whispers, loud enough that Seegs hears her, too.

Seegs and I stand up in the aisle, blocking Maguire from Lola. He opens his mouth and I want to rip into his A-plus teeth, deliver an overdue slap.

"I suppose she told you," Maguire says.

Yes, he towers over me, and yes, he's a goon, but the thing is, there's guilt in the way he says this—*I suppose she told you*—guilt mixed with something else—fear, maybe— and standing here in the aisle of the Darby Junior High school bus, I can almost smell the lack of confidence that Maguire is oozing, like the stingrays probably sensed in Lola. There's a sudden turn—I'm the sting-ray now—and I think I can actually solve this equation: boy + girl + twin brother + screw-up = trouble for boy! I'm a rational, problem-solving genius! I'm so wrapped up in the euphoria of solving teenage algebra that I barely notice Seegs push Maguire back up the aisle, or Maguire's reverse charge and head-butt to Seegs. The bus erupts in roars and cheers. The bus driver is yelling and pulls over to the curb. Seegs' nose drips blood like he's been hit by a ghoul engine in *Soldier of Fortune*, but he is smiling. Blood streaks his teeth. Lola flips through her backpack, looking for tissues or a gym sock, something to sop up Seegs' blood, but all she can come up with is a crumpled piece of paper. A rational numbers worksheet. I can make out Xs and Ys and squiggles, Lola's subpar handwriting. She rips the worksheet into strips and rolls a couple of plugs for Seegs' nostrils.

Maguire just stands there and stares at all of us for a long while. I wonder if he sees what I do—a girl who drinks Coke through cherry rope licorice, her crooked-scowling brother who has thirty-three teeth crammed into thirty-two sockets, a bloody action hero best friend who has overdue C-minus-quality math homework stuffed up his nose; a trio that makes no sense; a problem that no one like Maguire will ever be able to solve.

OUT OF SEASON

Twice a year, the 4-H people bus us out of our run-down suburb to show us another way of life full of pollinators and cow manure. That's where I meet you. Our eighth-grade field trip to the apple orchard and you carry bushel baskets up empty and back full, your jeans worn, seams faded to the color of ocean foam licking down your legs. You get the seal of approval from Vanessa. *Just the farm boy, but so hot.* Vanessa knows boys and knows hot, and so I know, too, by proxy. Maybe your name is Samuel. *I bet he's sixteen*, she says, and we robot-nod, filling our baskets fast for the chance to brush against you. In my frenzy, I pick up fruit from the ground. You take a bushel from me; you frown at the wormholes pimpled across my apples.

The wind picks up and Vanessa's hair whips into all of our faces. Her girl scent smells expensive, learned. You lean in to grab another bushel; Vanessa's hair spider-traps across your face. *This crazy wind. I just can't control myself!* Vanessa retracts her wayward strands, and you say *No problem* as if hair swallowing excites you, and then the two of you are off in the orchard. Your slurps and wet, wet, wet sounds broadcast beyond full bundles of ripe McIntosh. I bite into a sour Fuji and listen as the 4-H lady drones on and on about the dangers of a late spring frost. How can 4-H lady not hear you? Vanessa's shirt buttons misalign for the entire bus ride home to our dilapidated civilization.

At home, I pull out a smooth, pink-veined rock from the pocket of my apple-picking jeans. I'd found it nestled in the root of a Gala tree. It seemed logical at the time, pocketing that rock, imagining handing it to you—*Something to remember me by, Samuel*—right before I'd lean in, letting you know it was OK to kiss me, to sniff my ordinary girl smell. I'll rub that rock and dream of you, tonight, every night, Samuel. My decades-old, hand-me-down bed creaks for you.

In our potholed neighborhood, we ride our bikes until either nightfall or a cowbell or some mother's screech skittles us back inside. Vanessa toots her clowny bike horn the whole way home as if her whereabouts need any more press coverage. It's obvious to everyone that she's not long for this neighborhood, that someday soon she'll look at the skinny streetlights that protect our street and see them for the rusty, dim beacons that they truly are. Watch her as she drives her chrome-wheeled SUV away, Samuel. Your open palms extend to her in a half-wave, half-picture frame, your farm-boy face so special and then—there it is, faded. Out of season. But I'm still here, Samuel. Open your eyes.

WORD SEARCH

1. It shouldn't be so hard to say hello. That's the whole point of the word, right? To break the ice?

2. Urban legend has it that Alexander Graham Bell coined the "hello" greeting during the world's first telephone call to his girlfriend, Margaret Hello. I guess he was looking for something to say once she picked up. *Hello?* I imagine him asking. *Margaret Hello? Is that you?* As if someone else could have possibly been on the other end.

3. When I call you, you don't answer. Or you answer, but then you hear my voice, "Hello? Hello?" And then I hear, *click*.

4. The word "hello" is actually an alteration of "hallo," which itself is an alteration of "holla" and "hollo," all of which were 1800s shouts used to attract attention, kind of like "Yoo hoo" or "Hey there!"

5. Now that I think of it, your first words to me were "Hey there." When I looked up and saw you, your Italian horn necklace, Jack and Coke fizzing with lime, I wanted to bolt. I thought I knew your whole story

in those first seconds—West Philly, Madonna statue on the front lawn, chest hair for days. I couldn't have known it all, though. I couldn't have guessed.

6. The fact is, Alexander Graham Bell insisted that the word "ahoy" be used as the primary telephone greeting. By 1900, he lost out to his rival, Thomas Edison, and the word "hello." But Bell felt so strongly about "ahoy" that he used it for the rest of his life.

7. We sat barefoot, cross-legged on your front lawn, the plastic Madonna statue behind us. We devoured an entire bag of Chips Ahoys while Fourth of July fireworks blasted from city rooftops. Later that night— our first time. You loomed above me in bed and I saw it, too late to ask—the inky name engraved on your biceps. *Lucille*.

8. Mabel Hubbard was Alexander Graham Bell's girlfriend, not Margaret Hello. So the urban legend is false, unless Alex was two-timing poor Mabel? Seems unlikely that a man who championed the word "ahoy" would be the cheating type.

9. Maybe if you'd been my winter boyfriend—long sleeves, dark nights. But you romanced me with summer snow cones, weekends in Ocean City. *Lucille* exposed by concert tees; *Lucille* covered in sand and surf bubbles. *Lucille*, the other woman, the temptress with the name of a geriatric librarian.

10. If you answer the phone and ask me to defend myself, I'll say *Lucille* drove me crazy. I mean—Hello! Hallo! Holla! Hollo! You refused to explain.

11. I force myself to remember. That night I traced the loops of *Lucille's* Ls with my fingers while you slept; that night you swatted my hand away; that morning you left early for work and told me to stay, to sleep in, to hang out; that day I opened all of your drawers, cabinets, boxes until I found the photo albums; that photo that's so obviously you and Lucille, labeled "Halloween 1997"; that cowboy hat that dwarfs your head and squashes your curls; that Patsy Cline hair flip that frames Lucille's heart-shaped face; those bangs that highlight Lucille's moon-eyes, those eyes aimed only at you.

12. The mid-nineteenth- century British word "hullo" is deceptive. It was not used as a greeting, but rather an expression of surprise, as in "Hullo, what have we here?"

13. You use a more slang-y version of "Hullo, what have we here?" when you surprise me and come home early; dozens of *Lucille* photos litter your bedroom floor.

14. According to the American Heritage Dictionary, "hallo" is a modification of the obsolete "holla," as in *Stop!*

15. When you shout, the veins in your neck seem to stretch beyond the limits of your skin.

16. Lucille is dead. Lucille is dead. Lucille is dead.

17. The Italian word "ciao" is used for both hello and goodbye. Other words with this dual meaning: "sha-lom" in Hebrew, "salaam" in Arabic, "annyeong" in Korean, "aloha" in Hawaiian.

18. The last things I remember: you saying that we were only a slim beat away from being something, a slim beat, a slim beat; tear streaks on your bulging neck; words no longer words; the slick surface of Polaroids on the bottoms of my feet.

19. You will not answer the phone. You will not say hello or goodbye, ahoy or ciao. It shouldn't be this hard, but it is.

STEALING BABY JESUS

The night I stole the Baby Jesus it was fucking freezing. Twelve degrees or something. There was snow all over the manger, and a snot-cicle dingled from one of the Three Wise Men's heads. Anyway, the Baby Jesus was easy, a real grab-'n-'go, not like the rooftop Santa and reindeer set from over on Mission Street. That one was a real bitch.

I wanted to sneak the Baby Jesus up to my room unnoticed, but my mom hollered from the kitchen as soon as I opened the back door. "Matthew? Mark? Luke?"

"It's Luke, Ma." I shoved Baby Jesus under my Eagles sweatshirt and sidestepped into the mudroom.

"Luke, where have you been?"

"Out."

"Don't be a smart-aleck." Her wooden spoon clanged against the stainless steel mixing bowl. It was day three of her Christmas cookie marathon. I knew where that train wreck was headed—the dining room table covered with the same laminated red tablecloth and plate after plate of sugar-sprinkled snowflakes and Santa heads. Gifts for neighbors, teachers, the mailman, paperboy, Father Raymond, the nuns at St. Gabriel's, the homeless shelter on Fifth. Mom seemed to believe that the spirit of Christmas was giving.

"Hang up your coat. And take your shoes off—you boys are always tracking snow and mud inside."

"They're off, Ma, they're off."

There was no way I was going to make it through the kitchen all pregnant with the Christ child. His puffy toes stuck out of the bottom of my sweatshirt. They looked a little like Mom's amaretto cookies, just smaller and more plasticized. I lifted my sweatshirt and—pop—Baby Jesus landed Downey-soft into a laundry basket full of folded sweat socks and undershirts. I grabbed him by the neck and drowned him to the bottom.

"Geez, Ma. I try to do something nice and you're all over me."

When Mom saw me carrying the laundry basket upstairs her eyes twinkled like the six-foot light-up candlestick I'd nicked from Samson Street. Me, putting laundry away—a regular goddamned Christmas miracle.

I was eleven years old when I stole for the first time: swiped a life-sized Santa from our next-door neighbor's lawn. Mrs. Crawley was a witch. She never spoke, only snorted at my brothers and me in some kind of pig language. The Christmas my dad left, Mrs. Crawley put a mutilated macaroni-and-cheese casserole on our front stoop. Just rang the doorbell and left. Matthew saw her slink back into her house. Mom said Mrs. Crawley was nice, she just had a little social anxiety disorder. My brothers and I thought she was cursed and full of cobwebs. I wouldn't have eaten her mac and cheese for nothing. Anyway, I don't know what the hell she was thinking, sticking Santa in front of her mailbox. It was her only Christmas decoration, ever. She picked the suckiest Christmas on the planet to get some holiday spirit? It was three years ago that I took her Santa. Ma sent me over to drop off the empty casserole dish. I just left it on her stoop and took Santa as a tip.

"Did you hear?"

Missy Carmichael was on me the second I hit the sidewalk. She was seven, lived across the street, and thought I was Justin Bieber or something.

"Hear what?" I asked.

"Someone stole the Baby Jesus from St. Gabriel's!"

I tried real hard not to break step.

"Luke, are you hearing me?" Missy sounded all Cindy-Loo-Who broken up about it. "They stole Jeeeesus! Right from his crib! It's awful!"

"Oh, yeah?"

"It was on the news, and my mom said it was a sin, a bad one, and that whoever did it was probably going to hell and burning and—Luke? Luke, are you listening?"

I broke into a sprint at the corner of Elm and First. Missy never followed me past the corner of Elm Street. She was a good kid. A little too Baby Gap, maybe, which made her look like some stupid Sunday circular model. But she was good. Followed directions. Baby Jesus would be proud.

I snuck into the back of St. Gabriel's in the middle of the first reading. Leviticus again. Father Raymond was fucking obsessed with Leviticus. Gwyneth was there, four rows from the front.

"… then let him bring for his sin a young bullock without blemish unto the Lord for a sin offering."

My footsteps were squeaky from the slushy sidewalks. Goddamned people never shoveled any more. Weren't there laws about that?

"And the priest shall dip his finger in the blood, and sprinkle some of the blood seven times before the Lord."

I slid into a pew, seven rows behind Gwyneth. She was perfect. Her hair was blood-black, tied back at her neck with a hidden ribbon. She'd left her coat on. No scarf. Her neck must have been freezing cold. I wanted to touch it so bad, warm her face in my hands. I'm sure Leviticus would have something to say about that, probably make me cut my fingers off and smear the blood on a goat or something.

"Let us offer each other the sign of peace."

This was it. The thing I waited for all week.

Gwyneth turned toward me. Slow. Just like she would if we were alone somewhere together—in a car, a pool, a bed. She smiled right at me and bowed a tiny bit, like I was a human holy Eucharist. I gave her my best I'm-not-an-asshole grin, held my eyes wide open hoping they'd sparkle and not look too manic. Three, maybe four seconds of me and Gwyneth time. Luke and Gwyneth—Gwyneth and Luke. Someday I'd grow stones and sit right behind her.

Principal Stevens blasted us on the PA system before the homeroom bell. I tuned out as much as I could.

Baby Jesus stolen .... Not only a crime but a sin .... God's eyes upon the scene .... Return and no questions.

I thought about my frozen hands and how they didn't stick to Baby Jesus' bald head like I thought they would. I picked a booger, slimed it under the top of my desk. Gwyneth, of course I thought about Gwyneth. What a stroke of luck it was that day last fall, seeing her slip into St. Gabriel's, figuring out her pattern of Friday masses, knowing I could get close enough for her to notice me. I was going to get her, somehow. Without having to steal her.

Who would do this ... pray for all sinners ... God knows ... No questions. Return Him ... sin ... sin ... pray ... Sinners ... mercy.

The door on the metal shed stuttered something awful on its tracks. It was almost impossible to break into the damned thing without someone noticing. But I always did. Matthew was permanently connected to an iPod, Mark to a donut and reality TV. Mom was just not connected, period. The shed was packed with three years' worth of my Christmas loot, and underneath all of that was Dad's stuff – boxes of clothes, papers, books, Genesis and Pink Floyd albums, an old walnut chest of drawers he'd had as a kid. I used to sit in there right after he left, sit on the concrete slab floor and finger through his things, trying to feel something he'd once felt. Once in a while I could smell him; it was something like metal shavings and motor oil. But Dad was long gone from there now. I slid between the dresser and a candy cane-striped light post and nestled Baby Jesus at the top of the heap.

"Your dad is coming over tomorrow tonight." Mom was at the kitchen sink, trying like hell to scrub spaghetti sauce stain lines out of Tupperware.

"He is?"

He'd never been back to see us. Mom said he had a good job working steel up north with Uncle Tim. He sent money—mom stashed it inside the ceramic apple cookie jar on the kitchen counter. He called sometimes. Matthew and Mark talked to him, but when it came my turn, I'd be long gone—out the back, up on the roof, over the fence.

"Is he taking us out?"

Mom kept scrubbing. I could see her face in the reflection of the kitchen window, scrunched just like a scouring pad. "He didn't say."

"Fucking pointless."

"Ahem?" Mom turned to me. She always feigned a sudden loss of hearing when any of us cursed.

"It's pointless, Ma. The stain. It's there forever."

Her face looked full of lines, spidery cracks around her eyes. Dad did this to her. She turned back to the sink, resumed her rhythmic cleaning.

"Forever's a long time, Luke. I've got to try."

The last time I saw my dad was December 18, three years ago. I remember that because it was Mathew's birthday. Dad always made a big deal over Matthew's birthday, said it was because he'd almost died at birth, three pounds and moldy blue. Dad had had to baptize Matthew himself, gotten the OK from Father Raymond over the waiting room telephone. Made a vow to name all of his sons-to-come after the big-gun saints. Guess he didn't make a vow to stick around.

The birthday routine for Matthew that year was standard stuff. Dad drove Matthew, Mark and me over to the A&W for drive-thru root beer floats. Matthew sat right next to Dad in the front seat. Place of honor. Five large floats—the extra one was for Mom. She stayed home to clean up after dinner.

"What kind of cake did Mom make you?" Mark asked. He was the biggest fat-ass sugar eater I'd ever seen.

"Triple chocolate with coconut icing. Didn't you see it?"

Mark's face was intent on the flimsy plastic lid of his A&W float. He slurped the last of the milk-foamy root beer layer though the straw so loudly that Dad turned his head to the back seat. His coal-eyed stare landed on me. I didn't dare call Mark out for making the god-awful noise. Dad hated a tattler worse than a thief or murderer.

As soon as Dad turned his head back to the wheel, Mark snickered and grabbed the extra root beer float— Mom's float—and began to suck hard on the straw.

"Mark! Stop it!" I said.

Dad and Matthew turned around and looked at us. Mark was making his dopey cherub face, his cheeks Santa-red from all the vigorous slurping.

"What's going on back there?" Dad asked.

This was confusing. Dad had asked the question. If I told him the truth, was that still tattling? Mark stared at me, unblinking. And then he did the impossible. The fat fucker stuck his lips back on the straw and pulled a long, sweet stream of Mom's root beer float into his stupid-ass mouth.

"Mark is drinking Mom's root beer float," I said.

Dad just about stood on the brakes. We were in the fast lane of Walnut Street, which is practically a freeway. He threw the gearshift up to the North Pole and swung his door open, scraping its underside on the concrete median.

"Get out," Dad said.

He opened my door, stood there frozen.

"But Dad, you asked," I said.

"Get out, Luke, before I drag you out."

"But—we're kind of far from home."

He grabbed the arm of my parka, the fluffy stuff long-ago flattened, and it squeaked or I squeaked or something in my head squeaked when I landed on my ass in the median.

"What have I told you about tattling?"

Something about his face—the set of his jaw, the way it was knocked just right of center by some long-ago fight at the shipyard, or the way his icy breath just hung there after he spoke to me, blocking a clear view of him—something told me to just shut the fuck up, to sit on that goddamned median until the taillights of his Buick were two little cat eyes heading toward home.

A powder blue K-car in the right lane double honked at me. "Get out of the road, kid." A black leather glove stuck out of the K-car's window, waving me to the sidewalk.

Mom didn't say anything to me when I finally made it home. She folded me into her favorite Dutch Country quilt and held me tight, rocked me back and forth right there in the kitchen until my ears turned back into flesh.

Mark burst into the bathroom the next morning while I was brushing my teeth. "Gotta pee." He yanked his pecker out before I could spit out my toothpaste.

"Christ, couldn't you wait two minutes?" I spit the frothy crap out of my mouth—it looked like root beer float foam.

"Geez, you really hacked off Dad last night."

"It was your fault, Pig Boy, stealing Mom's float."

Mark shook his dick three times and shoved it back into his pajamas. "Yeah, well Dad wouldn't even talk to us all the way home. Told us to go to bed. No birthday cake, no nothin."

"What did Mom say?"

"She wanted to know where you were. I heard Dad tell her he was tired of all of us. Tired of her, too."

"Then what?"

Mark grabbed his toothbrush, overloaded it with gel until it oozed like cake frosting. "I heard the car start.

Matthew and I looked out the bedroom window and saw him head down the street. We thought he was going back to get you." Mark stuck the gooey contraption into his mouth and looked at me in the mirror. "Did he?"

I didn't answer him. While Mom had been warming me, I'd noticed the birthday cake still out on the kitchen table, uncut and whole, but I guess I didn't think about what that really meant. Our car hadn't been in the driveway. And Mom never used that Dutch Country quilt—it was a wall hanging kind of thing, and she never let us touch it. Clues. Big fucking clues right under my goddamned nose and I'd missed them all.

Things were different after that night. Dad was gone.

And now, Dad was coming home tonight. It was Friday, which meant it was a Gwyneth day. Things were looking up, except I'd woken up late, so I'd probably miss the first reading. I'd made it half a block from home before I realized that Missy Carmichael was running after me.

"Luke, wait up."

I didn't look back at her. "Look it, Missy, I'm really late."

Clack, clack, clack—I swear she was wearing metal spikes in her shoes, all the noise she was making.

"Luke, stop. I need to talk to you."

I didn't want to look at her. Dad always said you didn't ever look a stray in the eye, or else it might stick around. I figured the sounds of her would stop after I hit the corner of Elm and First, like usual. They didn't. I turned down First Street and I could still hear her following me. I had to stop and look. She was just a kooky kid, for Christ's sake, not an alley cat. She was thirty feet behind me. Her hair was pinned up on top of her head the way my mom did it sometimes before bed so that she'd wake up to a head full of waves. Mom never left the house like that, though. And Missy wasn't her normal color-coordinated self. Pink sweater, green pants. No coat.

"Are you crazy?" I asked. "You aren't allowed past our street, you know that. And where's your coat? You'll freeze."

Missy's eyes were all cow-swollen.

"Missy, you hear me?"

She started to cry. She was stuck there in the middle of the sidewalk, right next to the remnants of a week-old snowman. St. Gabriel's church bells rang. Mass was starting.

"Look, Missy. You need to go home."

It was as if she were propelled by jet fuel, the way she lurched into me, hugging me solid. After a couple minutes of mad sobbing, she looked up at me. "My dad is gone. He left us."

What the hell was I supposed to do with that?

"Look, I'm sorry."

She wiped her nose on her pink sweater sleeve. Father Raymond was probably preaching Leviticus by now.

"I thought you could … I dunno," she said.

I had a couple choices. I could give her my coat, take her back home, let her figure out the crap ahead of her just like I had—alone. That would work. Nice and easy. I might miss the sign of peace, though.

"You ever been to Friday mass, Missy?"

We walked into St. Gabriel's during the gospel. I think that's some kind of sin. It was the gospel of Saint Luke. The Prodigal Son.

I grabbed Missy's hand, made a beeline for Gwyneth. We sat three rows behind her.

"… Father, I am no longer worthy to be called your son."

"Who's the girl?" Missy whispered.

"What are you talking about?"

Missy looked about twenty years older and wiser than seven. "The place is empty. We're way late. And you drug us all the way down to the front, near her." Missy pointed at Gwyneth just as Gwyneth turned around. I wish I could have sunk into the pew, slithered down on top of the kneeler. But Gwyneth smiled at us, a wide smile with teeth, and there it was, a tiny wave, probably directed at Missy, who looked like she'd seen the Blessed Virgin Mary, and I knew that Missy was enchanted with Gwyneth, too. And somehow, it made me happy to know that it wasn't just me, that maybe Gwyneth did have some kind of secret power.

"… celebrate and be glad, because this brother of yours was dead and is alive again."

It was a kinder, more merciful Father Raymond. Come to think of it, he looked a lot like Frosty the Snowman, head-to-toe in white robes, his rounded head and goofy smile. His sermon was full of the promise of second chances, redemption, God's overwhelming mercy.

"Let us offer each other the sign of peace."

Gwyneth did the impossible. She glided out from her pew, genuflected, and walked right up to me. Next thing I knew, she was sitting next to me, grabbing my hand and then Missy's hand and smelling like strawberry shampoo. I followed behind her to receive communion. Surely it was OK, even though I was full of sin, because it was Friday and my dad was coming home and Gwyneth was saving me and I was saving Missy somehow.

"Sit next to me next week," Gwyneth said. Her skin was as white as the marble Virgin Mary. Her lips were glass smooth. She slid away, leaving me open-mouthed.

The cop car was waiting at the curb when Missy and I got back. An officer ran toward us, hand on his holster.

Get on the ground … don't speak … your rights ….

Everywhere there was cold—icy concrete, steel on my wrists, voices with none of Gwyneth's kindness. I wondered if they'd searched my house, the shed, found my stash of Christmas. Gwyneth would find out, she'd know that the holy Eucharist was burning its way down into my cursed stomach. Missy would know that I was the one who stole Baby Jesus, that I was not her salvation. And who knew what Dad would do.

The gravel in the sidewalk scraped my lips as I bargained—silently—to the Baby Jesus. *If You get me out of this, Baby Jesus, I swear to You, it's over. I'll return everything. Everything. Mrs. Crowley's Santa. The climbing elf ladder. The light-up wicker reindeer. Candy canes, jingle bells, everything. Including You, Baby Jesus. Especially You.*

Apparently Missy Carmichael had run away from home the night before and neglected to tell me. The cops thought she had been abducted—thought I was some kind of perv pedophile. That little shit Missy cleared me of all wrongdoing, called me a hero for finding her wandering the streets and taking her home. Mrs. Carmichael kissed me square on the lips. Missy gave me a tiny, sad smile. I figured she was in for some paddle time.

Mom looked worse than I'd ever seen her. She looked Mrs. Crowley old. Dad wouldn't like this, not at all. Me an almost kidnapper, Mom a hag.

"Well, I don't see why we'd need to tell your father about any of this." Mom stirred her coffee until she created a tornado vortex right in the center of the cup.

"But I didn't do anything wrong."

"Your father doesn't like any kind of fuss. You know that."

"I don't know dick about him."

I waited, but Mom didn't even react. I stared out the window, at the empty driveway lined with dirty snow and bike tracks.

The phone rang. Mom and Mrs. Carmichael talked for at least ten minutes. I'm not sure what they were saying, I only heard a lot of "uh huhs" and "thank yous".

"Looks like you're going to be on the news," Mom said.

"The news?"

"Mrs. Carmichael said Action News is coming tonight. They're doing a holiday feel-good piece—lost child, found child. They want you there, of course."

"Me?" I felt stomach acid swim upstream into my throat.

Mom smiled; she looked transported. Young. "Yes you, silly. You're a hero."

Hero. Me. Maybe Gwyneth would see me on television. Think I was hero material. Boyfriend material. I felt the scrapes on my face heat up and swell. Felt the bones in my wrists where the handcuffs had rubbed raw and tight. I had a shedfull of stolen Christmas. I was nobody's hero.

"You know, I don't think so, Ma. I mean, if Dad's taking us out, I don't want to miss that."

Mom stared into her coffee cup. "I'm sorry, Luke. Your father called again. He's just coming to clear his stuff out of the shed. He got his own place up north. He's not taking you boys anywhere."

I hammered my fist on the table and sent up a geyser of coffee from her mug. That prick.

The Action News van was parked in front of Missy Carmichael's driveway. I was supposed to be there by sundown so that they could interview us with all of the Christmas lights in the background. I would not disappoint.

The lock on the shed was jammed, and it took a whack with a plumber's wrench to set it free. I'd accumulated a lot of stuff. It was weird to see it all in daylight. It was probably what the Macy's Thanksgiving Day parade storage looked like, just way smaller and dingier. No one gave me a second look as I carted snowman after Santa after inflatable Rudolph across the street into Missy Carmichael's yard. Her dad had run about a million extension cords across their lawn for no logical reason; he probably was too busy thinking about splitting to consider his actual electrical needs. The Carmichaels' house only had three strands of lights and an inflatable Grinch in a bubble. Hardly camera-worthy.

It took me a good hour to finish the setup. The last thing I did was fish Baby Jesus out of the shed. Miraculously, I had never stolen a manger. I went back inside, walked right past Mom with the Baby Jesus in my arms. It's like she was catatonic—I swear she didn't even blink. I walked into the living room, grabbed the Dutch Country quilt from the wall and swaddled Baby Jesus until he disappeared in its soft blue and white squares. I took Him across the street, laid Him down at the base of the one-hundred year-old oak tree that Missy Carmichael loved to climb. I waited for darkness.

It was going to be spectacular.

NIGHT MOVES

Half of this story is true.

I drive to Wildwood with the shoebox strapped into the passenger seat of the Alfa Romeo. It's all that's left, and I will throw it into the Atlantic Ocean after dark.

The other half can't be true because I can't bear it.

Bob Seger's *Night Moves*. You play this same song over and over on the Alfa Romeo's cassette deck. I yell at you for all of the rewindings. *Can't we play some Van Halen?* Your dead-fish eyes do not blink; you play it again.

The true parts seem more and more like the not-true parts, the more that I tell them.

The police warn us to stay inside after dark. You open our screen door—*A little breeze won't kill us*. I insist we keep it latched. You're not scared of the hooded man. *I've got you covered,* you say, but then I wake up and your side of the bed is cold.

Truth is an ugly mirror.

You are into sex games. That's normal, right? But all of the time? When I ask you about it, you call me a prude. That's actually not true. You call me worse.

Sometimes lies tell on themselves without any help.

Your hands have cuts that you cannot explain. When you touch me, I can feel the tiny speed bumps of scabs on your fingers and palms.

Is a lie still a lie if it contains bookends of truth?

My favorite color is blue and so you grow delphiniums in pots on our three-by-five patio. You use a hunting knife to cut them into bouquets for me. I told you that the delphiniums smelled like summer, but actually they smelled like cat piss.

The not-true parts make for good alibis.

You're such a big man; surely I would've heard you if you'd left our apartment.

Not-truths smell like Clorox bleach.

Yes, I am beginning to wonder if, if, if. But as soon as I do, my gut seizes and I see you in your church clothes, helping your mom get out of the Alfa Romeo, your arms linked in hers as you stop to make the sign of the cross, holy water dripping through your curls.

Michele Finn Johnson

Tell the truth, the whole truth.

I do not show you the notes I'm keeping, but you find them. You ask me point blank, *Do you really think I could do this?* You are not blinking. I think fast. *I'm writing a book— the Atlantic City Strangler.* You burn my notes and tie me to the bed with our regular ropes, tighter though.

Nothing but the truth and a few non-truths.

You hang a rope over the hot water pipes in our living room. I cannot see this from our bed.

So help me, God.

You hang you. I will see this forever.

So help me, truth.

Sherry Gosling, Hannah Jones, Cindy Flannery, Cathy Moriarity, Kelly Flowers, Marsha Tomlin, Kimberly Daniels, Victoria Marshall. These are the names of your victims. They are true.

Some say I should add my name to the list, but that feels untrue.

They take everything from our apartment and label it as evidence. They take the Alfa Romeo.

Truth is a knot tied together with faithfulness, loyalty, fidelity.

When I get the Alfa Romeo back, it smells like a janitor's wet dream. They left a cassette tape, loose change, sunglasses that you bought on the beach in Wildwood, a few photographs of us. Everything else is gone.

Truth also means accuracy. Correctness.

One Bob Seger *Night Moves* cassette tape in poor condition. Seventy-two cents. Knockoff Ray-Bans, loose at both temples. Twenty-four photos in a flimsy plastic album from Fotomat of you and me in Wildwood last summer. You held me over top of spitting waves; you told me you were so happy you could die.

I choose to believe you were telling the truth.

They tell me it's OK for me to go back to our apartment, but of course, I don't go. I put the remnants of you into a shoebox except for the cassette tape. Side one, track two, is queued up. *Night Moves*. The Garden State Parkway is dotted with headlights. I push play. I don't push play. The truth, in this case, doesn't matter.

SANTO SPIRITO, 1577

My parents consign my eldest sister, Paola, to Venice's Santo Spirito convent. There is no dowry for Paola and so her duty is our salvation. When they took her away, Paola's nails dragged across the front door's casement, leaving ten tiny scratch marks.

To visit Paola, I have to walk through neighborhoods where the prostitutes live. I wear my moretta; I clench its button between my teeth, but no one seems to notice me anyway. I am never mistaken for an unscrupulous woman.

Paola tells me to stop judging people, that it is not Christian-like. I don't tell Paola that she looks like a stray dog with her nun hair chopped in uneven wedges.

The prostitutes wear yellow ribbons, but I can tell them apart from honest women by the cut of their gamurra, their scent of anise and smoke.

I ask Paola if she misses home. She will not answer me. I ask if the nuns have already removed her tongue, thinking Paola might laugh like she used to at jugglers and slow cows, but she stays silent for a long while. "I miss cigarettes," she says, finally. "Will you bring me some?"

One day I forget my moretta, and a yellow-ribboned woman tells me I look just like my sister. I think she is just a crazy woman, but then she calls me *tiny Paola*.

There are only two more months before Paola takes her final vows. She says I can continue to visit, but we will have to be completely silent.

My last visit before Paola is to take her vows, I hand her the bundle of cigarettes that I've smuggled inside of my gamurra. Paola grabs the cigarettes and slides them under her habit; she looks around for others before she speaks in a flood of words. She tells me about a tunnel under the walls of Santo Spirito, how the nuns crawl through it in the evenings, spilling straight into the yellow-ribboned parish; how she smokes and drinks vino novella until she stumbles; how she is keeping the company of several men. When we say goodbye, Paola's eyes close and her hands fold around themselves until they dissolve into her sleeves.

I walk home from the convent at dusk. I suck my moretta close to my face; I cannot be seen. The yellow-ribboned women look less like prostitutes and more like nuns with their hard eyes and raggedy hair.

I reach the edge of the yellow-ribbon parish, and I let the moretta drop into my hands. A strong breeze bangs against my naked face. It is dark when I get home—too dark to make out Paola's scratch marks on the casement. I reach out with my open palm, try to find some trace of something that I know for certain, but all I feel is the curved warp of oak.

GRAFTON HILL

Geoff says he's sorry, but he's not going to touch me tonight. My feet are on his lap and his arm weighs them down. He's doing that thing he does when he sprints—curling his lower lip above his upper, exhaling hair away from his eyes. Those eyes. They're half the reason I'm here, the way Geoff slants them toward me at running club. The angle of seduction, I call it. Geoff's been my sure thing for over a year. No strings. I root my toes around in his crotch just to see if he's serious, but he folds my legs into a V, sets them down between us on the couch.

"I'm surprised you called," he says. He stares at my hand. It's a pear-shaped diamond. Almost a full carat, but it's flawed. The colors from Geoff's TV reflect off its facets like a kaleidoscope.

"I always call ahead." I smirk at him. "You hate spur-of-the-moment sex."

Geoff leans away from me. "This is stupid, Mercy. You have to talk to me. For real."

The thing is, I want to talk to Geoff. I want to tell him why I said yes—it was an honest-to-God reflex, a reaction to the knee-bend and the jewelry box and restaurant cheers and then, *bam*! The holy-shit reality. I want to tell him why I'm sitting here with him, the most focused and logical person I know, instead of with my oopsy-daisy fiancé, but it feels wrong, all this sitting when Geoff and I are so much about motion—running, sprinting. Even our sex is about forward progress.

"Want to go for a run?" I ask.

Geoff's street is steeper than any we've attempted on our Saturday morning club runs—it's a nightmare triangle—and so I fall behind. I watch him as he jogs out up Grafton Hill, his shoes barely striking asphalt. He's a natural runner, not a forced one. Running's always been a grind for me. Just go. Move. No technique no matter how many tips I get from pros like Geoff who study this stuff. Now I see the flaw in this, my general lack of a life plan. Who would've thought spontaneity could lay such a trap?

At the top of Grafton Hill, Geoff bends and grabs his knees. He pants with an open mouth and waits for me to catch up. I'm glad to see this is hard for him, too.

"You trying to kill me with your neighborhood trek?" I ask.

Geoff reaches for me. I offer the hand without the ring.

"Let's sprint the downhill together." He squeezes my hand. "But at the bottom, you're talking to me."

The night air is cool, but today's sun is still radiating up from the street. We fly. I'm all legs. I force my brain to focus on pace and core position, and when we bottom out, I'm spinning in an endorphin high. Geoff stretches his calves on the curb. For a minute we stand on the curb together, pulsing our heels up and down, silent.

"I said yes."

Geoff is breathing like a metronome, even and controlled. "I didn't even know there was the possibility of a question."

There's a waver in his voice that could be hurt or anger, a fifty-fifty shot. Except I want to know, I want to be sure which way he is leaning before I decide if I'm going to tell him the truth or a lie.

"Why didn't we ever date?" I ask.

Geoff hops off the curb. "You've got to be kidding me."

He pulls me so close, I can feel his sweat through my T-shirt and on my legs. It's almost like being in bed with him, how his heat moves around on my skin, except in bed it's impossible to keep track of both his breath and tongue. Here, at the bottom of Grafton Hill, Geoff is both possible and impossible at the same time; if it's anger or hurt or fear or confusion that he's feeling, it is all of these things, all at once, inside me now. Wasn't it me who'd said, *Nothing serious? Can't be tied down?* Wasn't it Geoff who'd said, *If that's what you really want?*

It's something, the way Geoff's steady pulse has calmed me down. How my breath's returned to me. I reach around Geoff's waist and feel for that pear-shaped diamond. The point of it digs into the tip of my index finger as I turn it around to face the palm of my hand. I break away from Geoff and start to run, slowly, back up Grafton Hill. I count my footfalls, focus on smoothing out my stroke. My hair falls in front of my eyes and I exhale upwards, watch it fly.

MY VANISHING TWIN

Dead Twin Adam needs to get the hell out of my skull. It's like he's superglued in, a mini-megaphone inside of me. There's this thing called Vanishing Twin Syndrome—when a twin dies and the stuff it's made of gets resorbed into the other twin or the goop around them both. It sounds like total crap, but when you think about it, it sort of makes sense. Where else would it go? Anyway, lately, that's all I can think about, where the bits and pieces of Adam went. What parts of me are really only me? As sure as I'm sitting here, parts of Dead Twin Adam float around inside of me, including his pain-in-the-ass voice in my head. But Adam also flies around outside of me—living his life as a Mexican free-tailed bat. That part is, believe it or not, easier to deal with.

Mom cracks the eggs on the countertop. She lifts each egg over the mixing bowl, spreads their shells open with her thumbs. Whites and yolks dump out in strings and plunks. She told me yesterday that she'd make us a special breakfast—she had *big news*.

"You like Ernie, don't you?"

Ernie is Mom's auto mechanic. They started dating last year after the Kia threw a rod.

"Sure, I guess." Truth be told, Ernie has motorcycle hair and oily fingerprints. I want to throw him in the shower with a scrub brush every time I see him, and I'm not the cleanest teenager in the world.

"Don't sound so enthused." Mom holds the bowl against her hipbone; she whisks and whisks. Those eggs are going to be mega-fluffy, I can tell.

I pick at the corner of my placemat, flake off remnants of Lean Cuisine. "I guess I like the way you cook more whenever Ernie's around."

Mom smiles. "I do, don't I?"

I love when Mom smiles. It reminds me of the wedding photos of her and Dad that are jammed in the basement, two hippies with leaves and daisies woven into their hair, his hands touching her in every single photo, her smiles all directed at him.

"Well good, honey." The way she looks at me with mushy eyes, I know the road is paved for her big news. "You know you'll always be my baby, right?"

I sit back in my chair and flick my oversized bangs in front of my face. "Christ, Ma, I'm seventeen. Stop with the baby talk."

I see through my hair fringe that her smile is gone, replaced with Mom from the post-Dad era.

"Sorry, Aaron, of course." Mom rewhisks the eggs. "It's just that it's been me and you for so long, the two of us, and now …."

She pours the eggs into a skillet; she is making a hell of a lot of eggs. I don't know why I hadn't noticed it when she was cracking them, but the carton is open and all but two of the eggs are missing. Ernie has never been to breakfast before. Sometimes I catch him sneaking out of the house in the morning, grabbing his car keys and mumbling, "Sorry, kid." I like that about Ernie. I like that he feels the need to apologize for sleeping with my mother.

"And now it'll be you, me, and Ernie? Is that it? He's moving in?"

"That's almost it." Mom turns the flame on the stove down low. "I was going to wait for Ernie, but to heck with it." Her smile is back now, full force. Her face is flushed. "Oh Aaron, you're going to be a brother!"

Flash. I feel the heat of him before I open my eyes. It's not a normal heat; it's heat in motion, unpinpointable, a heat that zigzags. It could be a fly or something larger—a wasp, a hummingbird. But it's not. I know it's Adam by the erratic beat of his wings.

Come on, wake up, bro.

I look around my room at all the high places—my bookshelf, the ceiling fan, the curtain rod. I feel the bouncing waves of him tracking me, even when we're in complete darkness. At first, he's just a lump-of-coal-shaped shadow on my bedside lamp. I blink, rub my eyes and blink again. It is Adam—my dead twin brother—upside-down, suspended from the arm of my lamp.

Hey, Aaron. It's been a while.

Adam doesn't really speak—that would be crazy. It is more like a brain wave transmission from him to me—I won't call it a bat signal because that would be too trivial. He's my brother. He's a bat. And I can hear his voice inside my skull.

So we're going to have a baby brother, huh?

"I guess so."

Adam releases one of his legs from the lamp, scratches his sides and doglike face with a wing. *Is that why you called for me?*

I'd forgotten that I'd called out for Adam when I went back to bed without breakfast, telling Mom that it was a lot to think about, just the her and Ernie part, let alone some kid that would be my brother or sister— "Brother," she'd corrected me. "You'll finally have a brother." I already had a brother, I'd said, or had she forgotten? I heard her crying when she answered the front door; I heard her and Ernie mumbling, heard Adam's name.

I like the way you stuck up for me.

"Yeah, but I made her feel bad."

She'll get over it.

Will she, or will she check back into that crazy farm in Tubac, like after Dad left?

Plus, think about the opportunity—she'll be so wrapped up in that baby, you can skate a bit. Maybe you can get out of the whole homeschooling thing.

Adam has a point. I hate being homeschooled. Every morning I look outside the front window and see Jimmy Doogan and Pete McCreary walking to the bus stop, tossing a football back and forth across the street. They seem so normal, the way they talk, laugh, and throw the football at the same time.

Think about it. A new brother might not be so bad.

I leave my room around lunch—Mom left a plate of PB&Js and homemade snickerdoodles on the kitchen table. That is the thing with Mom—she tends to overcompensate. I hear the sounds of TV football. Ernie.

"Hey, kid."

Ernie sits in the La-Z-Boy as if he owns it. The La-Z-Boy was my Dad's chair—the only thing he left behind. I scratch both hands through my hair, punking it up until I can tell it's standing on end. "Where's Mom?"

"She ran out for a few minutes." Ernie points the remote at the couch. "Come watch with me. The Cardinals are getting thumped."

I can tell the game is in Arizona because the sky is so damned blue and it's November. The TV camera swoops in from the huge retractable dome onto the cheerleaders—half shirts, bare bellies, long legs shoved into white cowboy boots.

"Whoa," I say.

"Guess you don't see many girls like that around here," Ernie says.

I snort. "I don't think there's many girls like that around anywhere."

"Yeah, well you're probably right about that." Ernie sips his Pepsi. "But girls like that … they're not anything, really, compared to the real thing."

Ernie has a far-off look about him, a look that reminds me of Adam—like he is scanning the air for a blip of movement. "I know it's a lot to ask of you. Me and your mom, that's plenty." Ernie brushes the corduroy arm of the La-Z-Boy with his palm. "And now a baby brother. I get it, kid. It's rough shit."

I'm not quite sure where to look, so I stare at the tips of my All Stars. "Yeah. It kinda is."

"I promise, I'll try to make it suck less," Ernie says.

The television crowd erupts. Two Cardinals chest-bump in the end zone, and a guy with dreadlocks sticking out of his helmet dances a choppy dance.

"Oh, yeah," Ernie extends his hand up in the air toward me.

My hand feels so small against his, slapped in a high-five, stretched across the arm of Dad's La-Z-Boy.

Mom comes home after the game is over and finds Ernie and me asleep.

"Well isn't this a sight," she says. She sits down on the couch next to me, practically squashing my feet, and hands me a package wrapped in plain, brown paper. "Open it."

It is a double photo frame, thick brown oak surrounding two black-and-white photos. Ultrasound photos. On the left-hand side there is a little four-inch by four-inch picture, like one of those old-time Kodak instamatic camera numbers, black and white. The engraving below it says "Aaron and Adam—1995." In the photo, it looks like Adam and I are sitting in a barcolounger at the bottom of a well, butting foreheads. We look like we're lit from above, our heads rimmed with white halos, our skulls full of shadows. My brain looks like a brain; Adam's looks like a bumblebee. I know it's not a real face—Dead Twin Adam's—but he looks pissed off. Tight-lipped. The typing at the top of the photo says 'Twins—150 days.' Adam's eyes are a wide band of light, almost like he's wearing wrap-around Oakleys. It's creepy. On the right-hand side of the frame, there's a new black-and-white picture. The kid looks like a jelly bean. The engraving reads "Baby Boy—2013." I don't know what to say, so I say nothing. I look over at Ernie. He raises his eyebrows at me, which I take as man-code for, "Say something, Shithead."

"It's great, Mom."

She reaches over and grabs my hand. "You know I could never forget Adam."

I hear her exhale; she takes the frame back and walks it over to the fireplace.

"There!" Mom says. There is no avoiding that creepy photo of Adam and me now—it's front and center on the mantle.

Mom twirls the ends of her hair around her index finger. "Ernie thinks homeschooling's holding you back."

I look up from my biology homework. "Yeah?"

"He thinks maybe you'd learn more at Catalina. What do you think?"

Catalina High—a real school. Jimmy Doogan and Pete McCreary and cheerleaders. Mom looks like she's about to cry. I shrug. "I don't know."

Mom points at a diagram of the blood and circulatory system. "Look—what's that? There's two types of circulation? Pulmonary and what—systemic? I didn't know that—Aaron, I didn't know that!" She jumps up from the table, starts pacing in front of the stove. She looks like one of those sweat lodge heatstroke victims I saw on *Dateline*—beady and wide-eyed. I wonder if she's told Ernie about her time in the crazy ward in Tubac.

"It's OK, Mom, I understand it."

"Ha!" She slaps her hands. "No thanks to your stupid mom."

Mom leaves and I hear her bedroom door click. The sounds of Van Morrison—her depression music—float down the hallway.

I try and study but keep mixing up hypertension and hypotension. The graphs in my textbook blur together into circulatory shock.

Do it. Get out of here. Adam hangs from the kitchen track light; his bug-black eyes are fixed on mine.

I blink, rapid-fire.

Let's plan your escape.

The slow piano cords of *Old, Old Woodstock* soften Adam's guttural sounds. "Escape? I'm not trapped."

Adam swings around on the overhead lamp, one clawed foot hooked onto black iron, the other pointing straight at me. *Dude! She keeps you locked up in here, freakin' painting by numbers and listening to audiobooks while everybody else is off at football games, making out under bleachers.*

I think about Mom, late nights after working second shift at Raytheon, searching for lesson plans and free software trials.

Adam snorts through his piggish nose. *When you think about it, Aaron, it's kind of funny. I'm the one who died, but really, I'm way freer than you.*

When I walk into Catalina High, Jimmy Doogan looks at me like he knows me from somewhere. Everyone else and everything else is foreign. I try and look normal. *Pretend like you're in a movie*, Adam says. *The new kid is exotic, always gets the girl.*

"Are you new here or something?" Lizzie Montanaro looks like something out of a Katy Perry video—inky-black hair with fluorescent pink tips, spidery eyelashes.

"Yup." I grab a cafeteria tray and stand behind her, wishing I'd worn something other than overtly new Levi's.

Lizzie turns and looks straight at me. "Where'd you come from—wait, wait, don't tell me, let me guess …." She scans me up and down, stopping when she gets to my white All Stars. "Kansas, right?"

Lizzie turns and floats away, down the cafeteria line to the salad bar. Kansas? What the hell?

It's two weeks before I see her again. By then I've settled into a lunch table full of Biology Club members. They are mostly OK guys, although our table reeks of formaldehyde and egg salad. I'm halfway through a PB&J when I hear her voice behind me.

"Hey, Kansas."

I turn around. She's wearing a super-short denim skirt; the pink tips of her hair are flipped up into a curl. She smiles at me, and peanut butter sets up like cement in my mouth.

Swallow, you idiot. Tell her your name.

"Actually, my name is Aaron."

"Well, hi, Actually Aaron, I'm Lizzie." She points at the floor as she walks away. "Like my shoes?" she asks, pointing at a bright-white pair of All Stars. "We're twins, Kansas!"

I skip the bus and walk home. Lizzie. She's as far from my twin as humanly possible—she's so alive, and the way she's packaged—curvy but tight. Twins with Lizzie Montanaro. Imagine that.

I take a side road home, one that curves under Campbell Bridge. That's the first place I ever saw Adam. He'd hung upside down under the bridge, wings outstretched, while Dad told me he was leaving. I was nine years old and I thought bats were badass—they could fly, hunt all night, had sonar and sharp teeth. I knew a lot about bats. I didn't know a lot about divorce.

"Is this because of Adam?" I'd asked. "Was Adam ever actually born?"

Dad stuffed his hands into his pockets, tumbled coins as he tried to explain how Adam vanished from one ultrasound to the next, how he'd dissolved like a marshmallow when you sucked on it, how Mom disappeared, too. For some reason, I couldn't look right at Dad. It was easier to stare at the tiny brown bat right in front of us. The bat's wings were outstretched; he twirled around on one foot. Dad fumbled for words. The tiny brown bat moved closer to me, folding and unfolding his wings in slow motion, repeatedly, like some kind of code. *I'm Adam. I'm Adam. I'm Adam.*

Dad dropped to one knee. "Take care of your mother. You can do that for me, right?" I could tell he just wanted me to nod or say yes, but I couldn't. "She needs you twice as much, you see ... because of Adam, buddy. You get it, right?"

After that, Dad disappeared. Mom said he had a new family—two boys and a girl. They lived in one of the Carolinas.

The nooks and crevices in Campbell Bridge are empty now. It's February and the bats are deep into Mexico—Oaxaca and Yucatan—feasting on moths and flies. All except Adam.

"Can I borrow the Kia Saturday night?"

Mom's getting a belly. She touches it all the time even though she says she can't feel anything yet. "What for?"

"To go out."

I think I see her belly shift, just a little. "Go out where?"

Ernie pops around the corner, grabs an apple. He lives with us now, but sometimes I'm shocked to see his face in the house.

"I don't know," I say.

Mom laughs. "If you can't tell me where you're taking my car, you can't take my car. Simple fact."

Ernie reaches around Mom, puts his hands on top of the jelly bean. "Oh come on, Suzanne, can you tell me you and your friends knew where you were going every time you went out on a Saturday night?"

It used to gross me out, the way Ernie gets googly-eyed every time he touches Mom's stomach. At first I thought it was wimpy, but now—thinking about Lizzy and the scent of her bubblegum lip gloss, the way she almost sticks her tongue out when she smiles, how she laughed when she said yes to going out Saturday night, so full of giggle that I wasn't really sure it was a yes until she said yes—I'm starting to think that Ernie is perfectly normal.

I can tell Lizzie thinks that my choice of first dates—dinner at Chipotle and a walk under Campbell Bridge—is weird. But it's spring in Tucson, which means the bats are back.

"These really aren't the right shoes for this," she says, pointing at her flip-flops and the steep hill in front of us.

I reach for her hand. "Hold on."

We climb down a rocky hill to the bottom of the embankment and stare up at the underside of the bridge. "Listen," I tell her. Clicks and purring sounds come from under the bridge. The smell is strong—musky, like poop.

Lizzie's eyes are as wide and brown as Adam's. "Why are we here?"

"Just wait." Soon, the clicks and purrs turn into buzzing. Over our head, the bats start to fly—hundreds of bats summersault into the air and fly straight up, clouds and clouds of bats. None of them are Adam, and I am a little bummed—I want to show off, show him that I got Lizzie without him. The bats thin out and turn into pencil dots in the sky, and then I look at Lizzie. "Beautiful, huh?"

Lizzie smiles. "It's beautiful, Kansas!"

I don't know if this is how it's always going to be with girls, the instant vacuum of getting pulled into them, but I know that Lizzie is "it" for me—I know it like I know all the words to every song on Mom's *Tupelo Honey* CD; I know it by the way Lizzie absorbs my bat-speak, the way she listens, says "Oh wow" as I babble on about how bats are misunderstood, how they behave like families, how humans actually need them to survive. I am on such a high that I actually think for a second of telling her about Adam. But I know that is crazy.

Spring Fling night is only our fourth date, but Lizzie and I are about to do it in the Kia. Lizzie's purple sundress is somehow bunched around her calves and half of the steering wheel pushes into my spine. I am trying hard not to pant right into Lizzie's face, but I want to ask her if I'm OK to keep going and then—there he is, Dead Twin Adam, hanging from the rearview mirror.

Do it, Aaron. Don't puss out.

I freeze. Other than the bridge, I have never seen Adam outside of my house before.

"Is something wrong?" Lizzie's naked from the waist up, and the way her hair falls across her chest, she looks like a magazine photo.

You're the one who got to live—do this for me. Come on.

Lizzie kisses me. Everything about her is warm, soft, and a little sweaty in a good way, but everything about me goes cold. Adam? Here? Now? I haven't seen him in weeks and it's as normal as I've ever felt.

"Aaron, are you OK?"

You're OK, Aaron. You've got her practically naked.

I can't figure out how to speak. I'm sure I look like a pipsqueak Little League virgin to Lizzie. To her credit, she sits with me for what seems like an hour—probably more like five minutes. Adam is silent. Lizzie is silent. I'm silent. I just sit and watch her wiggle back into her dress and then walk away.

I'm not home five minutes before Mom's in my room. "What happened in that car, Aaron?"

Jesus Christ, she's like an enormous ADT security camera.

"Nothing, what?" I take a quick inventory. I'd put the Taco Bell bag in the trash. Lizzie wore some celebrity perfume, JLo or Jessica Simpson, and I bet it stunk up the Kia. Mom doesn't smell like that stuff, not even on date nights with Ernie.

"Don't go making me a grandma." She throws Lizzie's purple bra onto my bed.

I try to breathe without making any noise.

"I'm really not up for this." Mom's hair looks electric, over-Claroled.

"Ma, stop."

She stares at Lizzie's frilly bra. "I've asked Ernie to have the talk with you."

I hear the faint click of her bedroom door. *Tupelo Honey* wafts down the hallway.

Later that night, Ernie heads straight for the La-Z-Boy.

"You're freaking her out, you know."

"She's making a big deal out of nothing."

Ernie taps his pack of Camels on his knee until one cigarette leaps over the edge. He grabs it and holds it out to me. "Want one?"

"I'm too young for that."

Ernie laughs. "You're seventeen. Too young to smoke but old enough to screw?"

"Jesus, Ernie."

"She's your mother." Ernie shakes the cigarette at me. "You know how fucking paranoid she is."

"It's ridiculous. She treats me like I'm twelve."

"Ahhh," he says. "But you are, to her. Forever twelve." Ernie beats his palm with the filtered end of the Camel. "It ain't fair, kid. That bit with your twin." Ernie's eyes flash full of light as he pulls the Bic's flint trigger. "You've gotta do double duty."

Maybe Ernie isn't as full of gravel and gunk as I'd thought. "Nobody's ever said that."

He puffs a volcano of smoke over his shoulder, away from me. "Just do us all a favor and wear a condom."

Lizzie attacks me at my locker the next day.

"Aaron, did you find …?" She stops and looks around.

"Your bra?"

"Shhhh." Lizzie looks pink. "There are people."

There he is, Dead Twin Adam, inside my brain. *Screw with her.*

"I have it."

"Whew." Lizzie rests her back against a locker. She's wearing a tight white T-shirt, and I can see the outline of two super lacy cups.

Oh, come on. Dead Twin Adam stomps around in my head, his bumblebee brain's whirling. *What are you, a wuss?*

I clear my throat. "I'm not the one who found it."

Lizzie shoots up straight and bangs her palm on my chest. "What?"

"It must've gotten shoved under the seat or something."

Lizzie looks like she's going to puke. "What are you saying? Who found it?"

She pounds on my chest—thump, thump, thump, thump—and all I can think about is that dumbass ultrasound photo, Dead Twin Adam and me, our hearts beating in sync, at least for 195 days, our skulls mashed together, close as close can be. Would we have turned out that way, closer than close?

Way to go. Adam laughs, and I imagine his skull colored in brilliant reds—sunset colors—his eyes blazing white. *High five, bro.*

Lizzie's fear smells like crappy Walgreen's perfume mixed with gym sweat. She looks like she's about to cry.

"I'm just shitting you," I say.

"Jesus!" Lizzy hits me hard, right in the gut. "You're an asshole, Aaron."

She's got that right. Adam dissolves into the inner mush of my brain.

"And what the hell happened with you last night anyway?"

I look down at my All Stars, the front of the soles slightly separating from the toes. "I don't know."

Lizzie touches my biceps, gives them a squeeze. She sympathy-pouts me, as if I'd lost my dog or dropped an easy fly ball. "It happens sometimes," she says. "Stage fright."

It is exactly now that I know Lizzie Montanaro is from another world—some cosmopolitan place like Manhattan—a place that I could never be from.

"We're still on for Friday night, right? The big 'Meet the Parents' birthday celebration?" Lizzie walks away, doesn't wait for an answer. Her pink waves of hair bounce with every step.

When I get home from school, my bed is littered with college catalogs. Mom's obviously already been through them. Yellow Post-it notes peek out at all angles—happy faces, pointy arrows, exclamation points.

She really wants to get rid of you, doesn't she?

I ignore Adam and start at the top of the pile. Alabama. Mom's written a big "Check This Out!" with an arrow pointing to *US News and World Report*'s Top 50 ranking. Alabama. The Crimson Tide. It must be two thousand miles away.

There's a knock at my bedroom door.

"Come in."

Mom opens the door. "Looks like you found them."

I hold up a wad of catalogs. "If I missed them, I'd be too stupid to go to college."

She sits on the corner of my bed. "Aaron, you have so many options."

"I just always assumed I'd go to Arizona."

Mom irons the corner of my bedspread with the palms of her hands. "Ernie thinks I'm holding you back."

"Mom …."

"No, no. He's right. It's true." Her eyelashes curl into each other and milky black lines form at the corners of her eyes.

It's hard to breathe. What am I supposed to say? I wait for Adam. Goddamned Adam always has something to say, and where is he now? Who's the pussy now?

"Anyway," she says. "I've been collecting these for a while. There are lots of great options. Lots."

I can't help but feel I'm supposed to say something to make her feel OK. I scratch around in my head for some kind of words, but I can't come up with anything. I try to summon him—Adam? Adam?

Finally Mom pops off the bed. She kisses the top of my head. "You've got a whole year to figure this out. But you really should start applying soon."

That night, while I thumb through page after page of the best colleges that the East Coast, South, and Midwest have to offer, I hear Van Morrison, over and over again, pumping out of Mom's room.

Lizzie is at the door, all white teeth and ruby lipstick.

"Happy birthday, Kansas." she stands up on her toes and kisses my cheek.

"Thanks."

She brushes by me and I notice her short jean skirt, the one that will probably send my mother directly to Planned Parenthood.

"You must be Lizzie," Mom says. If Mom notices anything out of place, she sure doesn't show it. She gives Lizzie a three-second hug and next thing I know they are chattering about nail polish colors and the benefits of wedge shoes.

Ernie gives me a wink, nods toward Lizzie. He mouths the word "condom" and we both laugh.

"How many brothers and sisters do you have, Lizzie?" Mom asks.

"There's a lot of us—twelve in all."

Mom's eyes are full moons. "That must be quite a loud house."

"There's always something going on, that's for sure. And you can count on a line for the bathroom."

Ernie fist-bumps me. "Looks like they're getting along."

I look over at Mom and Lizzie, standing by the fireplace. Lizzie holds the ultrasound pictures, and I see Mom tracing the outlines of blurry bodies.

"I didn't know you were a twin, Kansas," Lizzie says.

Lizzie stares at the photo like it is some kind of complex physics problem that she'll never solve. I look up at Ernie, and it's like looking in a three-way mirror—me, Ernie, and my long-ago Dad—the light sucked out of all three of us as Mom babbles on and on about how exactly a twin vanishes—faulty embryos, in-utero brain anomalies, dead twin resorption. Honestly, I don't know why I thought this would go OK, why I didn't really think Mom would go crazy with all of the remembering that being pregnant probably brings back.

When Mom breaks out the birthday cake for me and an accompanying birthday cupcake for Dead Twin Adam, all of us look totally freaked out. "Make a wish," Mom says, lighting eighteen candles on top of my double chocolate cake. "And one for Adam, too," she says, lighting one lone candle propped up in the middle of a vanilla-iced cupcake.

I'm not sure what to do. Everyone stares. They probably think I'm having a hard time coming up with a wish.

Just blow them out, stupid.

Ernie looks confused. Lizzie looks gray.

Come on, the sooner you get this over with, the sooner your hands will be all up in that jean skirt.

Is he insane? Does he really think Lizzie is going to be horned up after spending the night listening to my mother obsess about a dead fetus—*his* dead fetus? Does he even know he is a dead fetus? Does he know what happens to people when Mom goes on her little dead fetus rampage? Does he know that people disappear? Real people, not just unborn people? Important people disappear forever, people like Dad and now probably Ernie and Lizzie. Mom disappears to Tubac. They all disappear. What psycho vortex did I pull Adam out of, and how can I stuff him back into it?

"Make a wish, Aaron," Mom says. She looks at Lizzie. "This should be easy."

I look at Lizzie, too. She looks as if she's gotten some really bad news; her bangs hang heavy over her eyes. She is disappearing. I close my eyes. I make my wish. I blow out my eighteen candles. I lick my thumb and my forefinger and snuff out Adam's.

The next weekend Lizzie says there is a safe place we can go and park. She's funny that way. No movie, no burger, no talking about my crazy mother and the dead fetus cupcake. Just park. This is fine by me. Adam's been silent after my birthday. I turn the Kia down a narrow, cactus-lined road; my headlights shine on a giant mesquite tree.

"That's where we're headed," Lizzie says. Her hand snakes its way up my leg.

"That tree?"

She leans into my ear and buzzes, "Mmm-hmm."

The closer we get, I can tell the mesquite is covered with something—graying tinsel or huge gummy worms.

"What the hell?" In the full headlights of the Kia, I finally see what covers the tree—hundreds of condoms. Condoms at car window height, condoms at the top of the tree, condoms on the ground.

Lizzie opens her door. "Let's get in the back seat."

As we get out of the car, I wonder how many of these tree balloons Lizzie is responsible for. She pulls out a Trojan from her purse. I don't need Adam to tell me what to do after that, but I do need a little help from Lizzie. She says that's normal, which again makes me wonder about her prior tree contributions.

We visit that tree a lot that spring; we make our own deposits until right before summer break. That's when Lizzie starts to speak to me in three-word sentences.

"I'm not sure."

"I don't know."

"Maybe—we'll see."

It only takes one look at Lizzie and Josh Armstrong standing together in front of Lizzie's locker to know that they are visiting the condom tree. Lizzie's back is against her locker; her fingers thread through Armstrong's belt loops. I get close enough to hear her say, "Oh, Josh, that's hysterical," to see her flash a slightly dirty prom-picture smile.

I'm not sleeping thinking about Lizzie and Josh, so I stumble in the dark toward the kitchen to make a PB&J. That's when I notice him—Dead Twin Adam camped out in Dad's La-Z-Boy. I blink twice. He is not a bat. He looks just like me and he's wearing my old Little League uniform—the Catalina Tigers. My tights ride way above his knees. I look closer. He is smoking weed or something that looks hand-rolled.

I'm thinking about going to Cornell, Aaron.

I'm not sure why, but the fact that he is talking to me stops me solid. His eyes look illuminated, kind of like the ultrasound photo.

"Why Cornell?"

She expected a lot from me. I can't keep disappointing her.

"What the hell are you talking about?"

All those years of fucking crying …. She practically what-if'ed me into Albert Einstein.

Adam hands me the joint and I take it, the paper and the heat as real as anything I've ever felt. "Don't be a shithead," I say. I fill my lungs with acidlike smoke, exhale slowly. "Day 195 you were off the hook, and I was fully on."

Adam groans. *You think so? You should've heard her— Did I drink too many PBRs before I knew I was pregnant? What were those chemicals at Raytheon? What if I'd never smoked? He could've been a baseball star. He could've been an astronaut.*

Adam's eyes glow—they fluoresce. He pushes the lever on the side of Dad's La-Z-Boy all the way down, way past center, past any position it's capable of reaching. His feet swing up and over his ass; his head aims down toward the living room carpet. He lets go of the sides of Dad's chair and hangs completely upside down, batlike. His arms are outstretched at his sides, his body no longer in contact with the La-Z-Boy. *Look at your baby astronaut now, Momma!* Adam's knees bend backwards, tuck behind him. His feet poke out from the sides of his head and he looks straight at me. *Cornell, buddy. Think about it. They have a great aerospace program.*

The college application essay is easy for me. I write about inner sonar—it's the kind of stuff that colleges gobble right up. I relate my life to bats—how they send out ultrasonic calls to decipher their surroundings, how they have to be able to separate their own calls from the echoes they receive in order to survive. Mom wants to read my essay but I won't let her. I know she'll take it hard—the bits about separation and freedom—and there's no point in her thinking about that stuff with the jelly bean on the way. Ernie said he'd take me to visit campuses, which will be cool, I guess. Nothing super far away. Definitely not Cornell.

I finish the essay and sit in the La-Z-Boy, push down on the lever as far as it will go, until my feet are at heart level. I close my eyes; all I can see are bats. None of them are Adam. Which gets me thinking. You know how when you are born, it's usually just you? You and all that gunky, ectoplasm-y stuff that had just been a part of you, but you had enough sense to shed it because you didn't need it anymore. But what about the bits and parts that you'd managed to absorb—months, days, seconds before that goop peeled away from you? The same stuff that is now medical waste was just millimeters away, molecules away, from making it inside of you. And now it's trash. What about that? What if the wrong parts had managed to squeeze through the membrane called "you," and the right parts, well, they were discharged into a red medical waste baggie and are on their way to the municipal incinerator behind Catalina High, the one that's so tall it almost begs you to climb up it? I think about this stuff. Yeah, I do.

RE-PETE

The doorbell rings and it is Pete. As far as you can tell, Pete + 5 years = Pete. Same close-cropped hair, same plaid shirt, same full lower lip. But when he speaks, you know that some things are not the same; some things likely left a dent, like your five-year-ago hookup with that coworker at your company Christmas party in the Sheraton coat closet while Pete waited and waited at his Camry until, finally, he came to find you, your back enveloped by a camel-haired trench coat that smelled of cigars and malt; that coworker, who Mach-3 bolted from that coat closet murmuring *Sorry dude* to Pete, who, in turn, drove you home and left, left, left you.

Now, Pete sits on your couch (same) and eats a dollop of homemade hummus (new) and drinks red wine (same). His legs are crossed (same) and he chews open-mouthed (same). Pete smells like apothecary cologne (new), and you can't help but notice that his nails are buffed, his teeth whiter, his shoes unscuffed (new, new, new). *You wouldn't believe it*, Pete says. *That move to Boston ended up being the catalyst.* You know and he knows that his move to Boston, January minus five years ago, was the result of an open-bar, top-shelf Absolut and tonic with lemon (corporate-appropriate quantity +3) Christmas party. Neither of you say this; Pete dips and dips into the hummus while he uses words like *success*, *millions*, *Europe*. You think that the word *millions* should make you moist; should fill you with regret like the blood sugar crash after demolishing a pint of Ben & Jerry's. You can tell that Pete is waiting for it, too—the reaction to his words, something more than a *Wow* or a head nod. But the sight of Pete on your tired, Ikea couch, his open mouth coated with caramel-colored chickpeas, instantly wears you out, like how you can only get three-quarters of the way through *Pretty Woman*, can't ever get to the part where Richard Gere stands under the fire escape to rescue Julia Roberts from her no-doubt-miserable, can't-make-it-without-you life, before you have to turn the whole damned thing off.

BIRTHMARKS

The tiny, rust-red mitten was imbedded in a snowbank on the side of Harmon Street. Cecelia could tell from the stitch—a cabled brioche—that it was knitted by hand, not mass-manufactured in China. Someone loved this mitten and the child who'd lost it. She peeled the mitten from the snowbank; it sounded like the rip of a Band-Aid. A few red fibers stuck to the ice. *The price you pay for being irresponsible*, Cecelia thought, looking over her shoulder at Harmon Elementary's playground. There were only a few kids outside, and they looked older than the mitten's likely owner. Cecelia considered the mitten, its size. First grade, second, maybe? She could never be sure—kids weren't her thing. Eddie laughed whenever she tried to talk to his children. *Get on the floor with them*, he'd say. *Just get in there.* Eddie was used to dating divorcées who had their own children. Cecelia knew the novelty of her inexperience would eventually give way to the questions—*Do you like kids? Do you want kids? Do you want my kids?*—and that would be her clue to move on. There'd been too many: the babies that didn't stick, the babies that stuck and then unstuck, the blue baby, the babies of her twenties that she'd melted away by popping two little, white pills. Cecelia held the mitten to her face; it smelled like road cinders. She pressed the crisscrossed stitches into her cheek, felt the yarn leave its impressions—dozens of tiny X marks that began to fade as soon as the mitten hit the sidewalk.

DARBY, NIGHTFALL

Dottie unlocks her bedroom window and waits in the dark for Bobby's taps. Lately he's startled her, his window taps coming long after she's gone to sleep. But tonight Dottie waits for him, vows to stay awake. She can hear the sounds of her mother in the TV room— phlegmy coughs, the snap of aluminum pull-tabs, burps. Dottie stares at her window screen. So far, it's been the only thing separating her and Bobby. He's been very patient. Tapping. Waiting. Window opening. When they say good night, they press their hands together into the spiky mesh of the window screen. The other night they'd kissed through it, Bobby's lips smooth and metallic. Dotty thinks this must be the same taste her mother always has in her mouth. Electrified tin. Dottie wonders why it is always like this with Bobby, the darkness, the tapping. Why in the hallways at school Bobby turns away from her. *Who'd live in Darby dump*, she'd heard the other day, said to Bobby, but not directed at Bobby. Bobby is an Ardmore boy. Bobby doesn't have to wait for much. He won't wait forever. Dottie unlatches the screen, pulls it to the floor.

SAVE US FROM EXTINCTION

The pillar stands in the middle of Town Square, a monument to dead soldiers. I sit beneath it and wait for Alesia, staring at the huge plaque of names. Alesia is late. Probably had to lie to her dad, say she was meeting Hannah or Katie at the mall. Her dick dad has it in for me. He hasn't said so; actually, he's never done more than snort at me, *Have her home by nine*. Alesia says it's not me. *He's haunted. You … well, you remind him of my brother*. I search the plaque until I find him—Rogue Robinson. Afghanistan. Alesia said he'd gotten blown up running into a building to retrieve the body of a dead soldier. *No man left behind*, she'd said, except the way she said it, it sounded like a curse. I stopped going to Alesia's house after I saw the picture of Rogue hanging over her fireplace. It was spooky—my same protruding jaw and caterpillar eyebrows, same nostrils shaped like jelly beans. I asked Alesia if she saw it, too—if she thought it was weird, or if what we were doing together was hillbilly-gross, but she just stuck her hand over my mouth. Shush. I nibbled her fingers—she tasted like an Almond Joy, and I stopped thinking about Rogue, started thinking about Alesia, how her hair feels like rain when it slides across my belly; the way she counts the seconds—out loud—while I unsnap her bra (my record is four). *You dinosaur*, she'll say, if I ever go past ten. I'm pretty sure I love Alesia, so I need to get over this Rogue look-alike business. He has a Purple Heart, but Alesia and I have blood-pumping hearts that are in almost-love, and I have to believe that this is something Rogue would be totally OK with, even if his dad isn't. And Rogue's dad—I know I should cut him some slack; his only son is dead. The end of his family name.

Alesia texts me—*b there in 10, T-Rex!*

The wind picks up and I move to a bench behind a stand of evergreens. I stare up the pillar to the statue at the top—an anonymous soldier, his cargo pants permanently puffed out, pockets full of marble grenades, his backpack burdened with the weight of rock. The soldier has a firm jaw, set square like Rogue's, like mine. He faces into the wind, unflappable.

THE CONSTANT NATURE
OF TOXICITY

Thirsty Girl cannot get enough fluids. She drinks and drinks from the porcelain water fountains at school—arcs of water like playful whale exhales, constant water flowing in the linoleum hallway, and then, after numerous scoldings and tiny folded warning letters from the Sisters of the Immaculate Heart of Mary that are sent home to Thirsty Girl's parents, Thirsty Girl begins to drink from an orange Coleman water jug like the kind used by I-95 construction workers, the jug ever-present next to her desk, hooked to her mouth with IV tubing, and Thirsty Girl drinks and drinks during endless bouts of long division, her classmates carrying the one and subtracting nine, all the while Thirsty Girl's face changes before them daily, the hallows of her face ballooning with hydrogen and oxygen, bonding together and forcing their puffy molecular structure into and around Thirsty Girl's bones, and the other children begin to call her names under, and then on top of, their breath, *Marshmallow*, *Bean Bag*, and of course, *Miss Piggy*, and Thirsty Girl cries—how could she not—and her tears run through the valley cut between her cheeks and her nose into the corners of her mouth, and she drinks those, too. The orange Coleman jug empties at such a frequency that the Sisters of the Immaculate Heart of Mary can no longer take it, the refills on the hour and then the half and quarter hours, the endless bathroom hall passes, the unprecedented carte blanche hall pass that, ultimately, threatens to derail the entire Immaculate Heart of Mary system, which, in turn means that Thirsty Girl will be, finally, sent home for good.

Doctors are, of course, consulted. Everything is toxic, they say. It is a matter of dose. Diuretics are employed to empty her. Thirsty Girl becomes thirstier, if that is even possible. Thirsty Girl no longer fits into the family vehicle; her feet and arms are carnival balloons. *Am I toxic?* she asks, and while her parents shake their heads *no*, she can see that the pails of water have stretched out their arms, that their shoulders are out of socket.

Thirsty Girl's parents are not, as you can imagine, equipped to deal with the demands of Thirsty Girl. They do the best they know how—her father, an engineer, creates a roundhouse of orange Coleman water jugs and IV tubing, and Thirsty Girl sits in one place in her bedroom. The IV tubing mechanically reorders itself and provides Thirsty Girl with a constant supply of water, until the relentless nature of it, the filling of the orange Coleman water jugs, brings such misery upon Thirsty Girl's parents that they, in a fit of fury and of problem solving, take to the backyard and dig and dig until they reach the end of it, the end of soil and begin-ning of the stuff of the planets—a bowl of rock, a solidi-fied magma pool—and they fill the pool with the garden hose, sit Thirsty Girl by its side, Thirsty Girl now the size of a Macy's Thanksgiving Day parade float, and Thirsty Girl drinks and drinks, a smile occasionally eclipsing her monsoon-swelled face, and she drinks from the magma pool using galvanized culvert piping, the pool draining faster than the garden hose can produce. Thirsty Girl's parents battle rights-of-way and water rights and dig a canal, the Schuylkill River now cutting through to Thirsty Girl's backyard; the headwaters of the Atlantic pulse life into Thirsty Girl's pool, and now a constant flow of water weighs into Thirsty Girl, and the swelling mass of her scoops its way into the Earth, a burrowing version of Thirsty Girl, a waterlogged beetle tunneling her way, at last, below the crust, her thirst waning from the weight of it all, the pressure of the soil on top of her and the water inside of her combining into something else, something all consuming, until the constant nature of the thing that sates her is, at last, toxic.

CRUEL SUMMER

Violet and Paula sit next to each other, cross-legged in the mink-lined nest. In life, both Violet and Paula were much more practical—cotton washables, handbags from Target, generic-brand girls—but up here in the clouds, they fancy themselves a higher-class species.

☾

Carla knows Sam is cheating again—late nights at the office, covert loads of laundry. A part of her doesn't really care. What's one more loss this year? If she could get through last summer, losing Mom and Paula, she could get through anything. Carla's cell buzzes. Sam. *Running late*, he texts.

☾

Paula stands up in the nest, tilting it off balance. "What is she thinking? Leave him!" she screams.

Violet pulls Paula's kneecap as if it were a joystick, steering the nest upright again. "You know Carla; she's like a kettle. When she boils, she'll boil over."

Paula swats Violet's hand away. "That's the new Carla. Old Carla would have bit him in the nut sack."

☾

Carla thinks she smells some cheap-ass celebrity perfume, Jessica Simpson or J. Lo, when Sam climbs into bed at 1 a.m. She moans at the nasal offense.

"You OK, baby?" Sam asks.

Carla just lies there—*Am I OK? Am I OK? Am I OK?*—until her radio alarm clock sounds. Bananarama's "Cruel Summer." She remembers dancing with Paula on the hood of Bobby Rosano's car, Paula with that floppy straw hat she'd bought on the boardwalk for seven dollars. She'd worn it all summer; they'd danced as if there were a proper floor beneath them. If one slipped, the other grabbed.

☾

Paula leans back in the nest, her legs draped over Violet's lap.

Violet puts down her knitting needles; she's making a spider-silk lap blanket for Carla even though she knows she can't deliver it.

"What are you gloating about?"

Paula smiles. "Promise not to ground me if I tell you."

Violet thinks hard about pushing Paula out of the nest, letting her find her own space in the clouds. But then she remembers Carla off to college. Carla off to her first job. Carla off to Sam. The loneliness.

"For the love of mighty Christopher, just tell me."

Paula holds up her hand, tunes an invisible dial. "I've figured out how to control Carla's radio."

☾

Carla unplugs her radio and plugs it back in. Reboot.
Bananarama again. *For the love of mighty Christopher*, she
says out loud to no one. Her mother's 1940s form of
cursing. Carla remembers her mom at the end, her last
words. *Be happy*. She unplugs the radio, leaves the cord
stretched across the floor like a snake. She hopes Sam
will trip. Hit his head. Reboot himself.

☾

Violet finishes the last stitch on the spider-silk
blanket. She looks at Paula, huddled in the far corner of
their nest, knees pulled to her chest. "It will be all right,
dear," Violet says. "You'll find another way in."

Paula throws her hands up in the air. "That was it!
That was the way!"

Violet knows Paula is upset about the unplugged
radio, but she also knows something that Paula doesn't—
Carla's thoughts; she knows *Be happy, Be happy* is ratting
around Carla's mind like an egg on an uneven table; it's
just a matter of time before the whole thing cracks wide
open and for the best.

Paula rubs her legs like kindling. "It's freaking
freezing up here."

Violet wishes she could reassure her somehow—
Paula was so young when she passed, her love line a
wide-open sky. Violet stretches the spider-silk blanket
across Paula's lap, watches as her goose bumps recede.

WHAT REMAINS

The fog was so thick, Jolene couldn't be sure that the figure in the doorway was really her father. It looked so much like Mo, but the thing was, he'd died in 1978.

"I'm glad you didn't move," Mo said.

Jolene held onto the door jam to brace herself. His thunder-crack voice.

"Don't mind if I look around, do you?"

Jolene blinked rapid-fire, looked toward the bottle of merlot to find its meniscus. Three quarters gone. Mo poked at a bookshelf, slid a bony finger across the spines.

"Do you want to sit down?" Jolene stopped herself short, didn't call the man "Dad."

"Everything looks so different," Mo said.

Mo had that same look about him that he'd get on their family trips to the Albuquerque state fair; exasperation with something or other—the summer heat, backseat quarrels, Mother's squawks about Mo's heavy braking.

"It's all pretty much the same, I think."

Mo pointed at the sectional couch. "That? You think that's the same?" The flat-screen TV above the beehive fireplace. "That thingamajig?" Mo zigged and zagged throughout the living room, intermittently touching post-1978 objects and throwing his twiggy arms up into the air.

Jolene couldn't stop looking at Mo, the way he seemed spun out of both skin and clouds.

"Is there something in particular you're looking for? Can I help?"

Mo increased his momentum of exploration, now moving at the speed of a New Mexico dust devil.

"Dad?"

Jolene felt the chill all at once as Mo reached for the copper urn that contained her mother's remains. Mo turned toward her, lips moving. He mouthed something over and over, the same words, but his thunder-crack voice was gone. His lips and face and frame melted slowly, like cotton candy on a wet tongue.

HOW TO SURVIVE A
NUCLEAR MELTDOWN

The ghost who inhabits my powder room is a thermodynamic anomaly—she generates an enormous quantity of heat versus radiating the chill commonly associated with the spirit world. My real estate agent and I noticed this wild temperature swing during our pre-purchase walkthrough, but the home inspector said it was just an HVAC system imbalance and to close the vent. No luck. Stay in that powder room long enough, and you'll swear you're going through menopause, but from the outside in.

The ghost's name is Edith. My grandson, JJ, talks with Edith frequently now that he can fly solo for his number ones and twos. JJ says Edith makes him laugh. *She tickles me, and my pee comes out fast!*

JJ sits on my lap for story time; he paws at my gaucho pants.

"Edith wears Lulu Melons like Mommy."

His mommy—my daughter-in-law—freaks if I give JJ a french fry. I'm not her first choice for babysitting, but I'm her best choice ever since I retired from the power plant and moved two blocks away. She knows motherhood's not my strong suit; I'm much better at fixing nuclear core meltdowns than the toddler type.

"Let's keep Edith between you and me, OK, JJ?"

The exorcist I hire off of Craigslist says the best chance for success is on the eve of a solstice. Is it smart to wait three months? I answer the exorcist's emailed questions—No, Edith isn't causing anyone harm; no, Edith isn't creating any physical property damage; yes, Edith's staying put in the powder room. *Sounds like the perfect houseguest,* the exorcist replies. We set a date in June.

My daughter-in-law calls in a panic—JJ has a fever and can't go to daycare. Can I keep him today? She drops him off with a thermometer, temperature log, and written instructions on administering his meds. I'm measured with my affirmations to her—*Understood. Of course. Yes, I'll set a timer*—acutely aware that she's scanning my kitchen for toxins like gluten and cane sugar.

JJ paddles down the hall toward the powder room. "Can I visit Edith?"

My daughter-in-law scoops him up, gives me a look. "Who's Edith?"

I take JJ from her. "That's our secret code for going potty."

"Later, my dove," I whisper into JJ's bangs, measuring the temperature of his forehead with my lips. "My, that's quite the fever!"

☾

JJ's clammy and gray; his fever will not break. His napping head numbs my lap; I tell myself that, in the future, I will not be quick-tempered when JJ butt-sleds down my staircase or repeatedly opens and closes the refrigerator door.

The timer goes off. In goes JJ's thermometer: 104 degrees. I look at my daughter-in-law's temperature log. His fever's been climbing steadily for hours. She didn't give me a limit—a panic number. It's been thirty years since JJ's father was a toddler, but 104 sounds bad. Dangerous.

"JJ, let's get up and go potty. Then we're going for a ride."

JJ sits on the powder room toilet, but he's so woozy, I have to hold him steady. Come to think of it, I'm pretty lightheaded, too. No breakfast, half a bagel for lunch. Christ, the heat in this powder room—even with the door open to the hallway, it has to be ninety-five degrees in here. It feels like my old control room in the power plant, so close to the generating cores, I found it hard to believe I wasn't being irradiated, no matter what the safety meters said.

"Come on, JJ, make a tinkle for Nana."

"I don't wanna."

Urgent care or ER? I should probably call and ask my daughter-in-law or face the wrath of a wrong decision.

JJ points at something behind me. "Edith says we should stay home."

Every hair of mine, even those on my legs, is electrified. Is she trying to kill my grandson? Maybe the Craigslist exorcist makes emergency house calls.

"Well, then, Edith must not be a mother, because she'd know a little boy with a high fever needs to go to the doctor's."

JJ starts to laugh; he kicks his heels and swats at the air—"Stop! Stop! It tickles!"—and the stream of pee we've been waiting for comes out in a torrent.

I rip a couple squares of toilet paper off the roll and dab JJ dry. Sweat beads bloom across his forehead.

"All better now!" He giggles, blows kisses to the back wall.

I lay the back of my hand against his cool, damp forehead. Edith—a steaming ghost—out-mothered me.

JJ stares at me with the look his mother has perfected—composure combined with an equal measure of disdain. "Edith says you were mean. Edith wants you to say you're sorry."

Edith's right. When did motherhood become a competitive sport? When did bettering each other become the goal?

"I'm sorry, Edith."

Intense heat rises up from my toes to my head, like a controlled fission reaction. JJ's turning blurry. My eyes grow leaded; they close.

"Edith will make you all better, Nana, just like she fixed me."

Something, someone, begins to pat down my damp, thinning hair. My mother, putting me to bed when I had the mumps. Patting, patting. My free hand grasps hers—everything arrives from long ago, all at once. Mother, coaxing me to sip cola-flavored medicine from an icy spoon. Mother, rolling cool washcloths, draping them across my forehead. Those papery fingers. The thinnest of heartbeats. I want to hold onto her forever, memorize her framework, but then she finds it—the tickle spot hidden at the edge of my ribs. She wriggles her knuckles into me until I crackle with laughter.

"Nana better now?"

Coldness surrounds me; my core's filled with control rods sucking the fever right out of me.

"Magic words, Nana?"

"Thank you, Edith."

JJ pokes at my nose, splatters my cheek with wet kisses. His puppy breath's so pungent, so cool against my face. So keenly alive.

DEVELOPMENT TIMES VARY

Preston Goodman was the Holy Grail of Walton High in 1984—junior class president, rugby star, all-around hottie. I watched him. I watched him in between second and third periods when he stuffed books in his locker; I watched him in the cafeteria sitting with the rest of the rugby team; I watched him climb into his midnight-black Trans Am at the end of the school day. Of course he didn't notice me—there were no huge spotlights pointed on flat-chested, frizzy-haired misfits. Preston, however, glowed golden under Walton's metal-halide stadium lights. He looked like one of those saints they baked into stained glass, which was how I thought of him until the day he showed up at my open period oasis—the abandoned athletic equipment-turned-pothead-hangout shed—and lit up a joint. What was he doing there? I couldn't breathe. I picked up my flat feet and bolted to biology lab, visions of Preston and pot and ruined perfection spinning in my brain.

I prayed for an easy lab, one where we looked at rolled-out screen prints of frog cross-sections or cow eyes while Mr. Potter, our apple-headed teacher, blabbed on and on about endocrine systems or cell division. But unfortunately, Mr. Potter had moved onto the topic of the human brain.

Sammy Springer, my lab partner, was already at our bench when I got to class. He was playing with a plastic skull and color-coded rubber brain lobes.

"You smell like weed," he said.

"Pfffft," I blew artificial smoke at Sammy's nostrils.

Sammy threw the green temporal lobe at my head.

Mr. Potter slapped his hand on the front desk. "Today we will explore the most fascinating and complex organ in the human body—the brain. I'd like you all to look at the replica on your benches. Note how all of the colored sections—the lobes—fit together."

Sammy held the two sections of plastic skull together and lifted it up toward the overhead lights. "Well, would you look at *that*!" Sammy pointed at a side view of Carlton Spencer, who sat at the lab bench in front of us.

"What?" I looked at Carlton but saw nothing remarkable. He was Walton's star baseball pitcher, but surprisingly he was not deemed cool. He was too skinny, quiet, and smart to be cool. He also had some rather unfortunate deterrents—a hooked nose, sallow, pockmarked skin, ever-present parachute pants. Carlton would pitch, we'd win, and all that he would get from his teammates and in the hallways were respectful nods. Rocko, the catcher, told me he never looked Carlton directly in the eye. Ever.

"This skull has the same Klingon ridgeline as Carlton!" Sammy said.

"Sssshhhh," I said. Mr. Potter was mostly deaf, but not totally out of hearing range.

Sammy pressed both halves of the skull against his head, hands clasped over the plastic ears. "Look at me—I'm Klingon Carlton," he declared, loudly enough for Carlton to hear.

Carlton whipped up off of his lab stool, his face as red as a watermelon Jolly Rancher. The stool slid out from under him, landed with a metallic crash.

"What's going on here?" Mr. Potter asked, both hands on his sweater-vested hips.

Before I knew what I was doing, I hopped into the aisle and tried to get between Sammy and Carlton. Sammy came up behind me and shook me off. I fell on my ass.

Carlton rushed past me, mushed himself into Sammy. "What did you say?"

"I'm Klingon Carlton, Plastic Man!"

Carlton swiped the back of the plastic skull with his open hand. It was his pitching hand, built for speed and precision. Skull halves went flying, and pieces of it were discovered long after we'd left vulcanized brain parts behind and moved onto dissecting worms and fetal pigs. Sammy got suspended for three days—it was his third demerit of the semester. Carlton and I ended up with the same punishment, harvesting fruit flies in Mr. Potter's lab after school.

"Everyone thinks that fruit flies are a nuisance, a pesky insect to be killed."

Mr. Potter began his after-school lecture before I even had the chance to take off my backpack. I sat down next to Carlton at the front lab bench; he didn't look at me.

"In reality," Mr. Potter continued, "everything we need to know about human beings, how we are formed, how we transform from embryo to fetus, from fetus to baby, from baby to adult, well … it's all here, in this glass." He picked up a small glass jar the size of a baby food container and held it out toward us as if it were Exhibit A of some very important trial.

"I think he has tears in his eyes," I whispered.

Carlton half-smiled.

"Follow me, you two." Mr. Potter headed toward the lab hood. Inside the hood, there were a few dozen empty bottles of varying sizes, short and tall pipettes, a jar of milky liquid, and a penlight.

"Today we will start a new civilization." Mr. Potter grabbed a tiny pipette and the jar of milky fluid. He slid the fruit fly jar to Carlton.

I leaned over to look inside of it. It was hard to see what was going on in there.

"Pay attention, because you two will be doing this by yourselves until you fill up all of these jars with about 100,000 fruit flies."

Carlton turned to me, unblinking. "It could be a long semester," he said. His eyes were Dairy-Queen swirled, gray with blue.

"OK, almost ready …." Mr. Potter carefully metered white liquid into the pipette, controlling the flow by flapping his thumb open and closed over the opening.

"What is that stuff?" I asked.

Mr. Potter didn't respond. His eyes focused on the meniscus inside of the pipette. Even his fuzzy nose hairs seemed erect with concentration.

"Yeast, I think," Carlton said.

"That's right, Mr. Spencer. I can see you've been studying. Ms. Finch, you could learn a thing or two from your new lab partner."

"Why aren't we using fruit?" I asked. It seemed like a logical question, but the lines across Mr. Potter's brow suggested otherwise.

"Too smelly," he said. "OK, Mr. Spencer, close the lid and hold up our specimens, nice and steady. Ms. Finch, pick up that penlight and aim it at the bottom of the jar."

I moved closer to Carlton and flicked on the penlight. The jar was alive with caramel-colored flies, each the size of a dull No. 2 pencil point. There were pockets of yellowy eggs, sand-colored sacks that Mr. Potter called larvae, and thicker sacks called pupae that each held the outline of a fly.

"You will have more flies by tomorrow, and they'll be hungry."

"How quickly do they multiply?" Carlton asked.

"Development times vary. They are ectothermic creatures, so the warmer it is, the faster they multiply."

Carlton looked over his left shoulder at his bat bag, plump with baseballs.

Mr. Potter continued. "These little guys just need some heat and nourishment, and you'll be surprised how quickly you two will be through with your punishment."

Carlton cleared his throat. "That's good, sir, because Coach Rusty wanted me to talk to you about practice."

Mr. Potter looked over his thick black rims at Carlton. "Surely Coach Rusty doesn't think I would do any special favors for his players?"

"No, Sir." Carlton ground his right sneaker into the linoleum floor.

"Move that light closer to the bottom of the jar, Ms. Finch."

As I moved the penlight, the flies congregated, formed a splotch.

"See, they like the heat," Mr. Potter said. "Now move them away from the food bowl." There was a tiny little saucer the size of a Barbie hat mounted on the bottom of the jar. I slid the light over, and the fruit flies followed.

"You're like the Pied Piper," Carlton said. We laughed. Our heads were so close, I could smell sunflower seeds on his breath.

"Mr. Spencer, slowly open the lid." Mr. Potter aimed the yeast droplets at the saucer. "Use one 2 cc pipette per jar." Mr. Potter emptied the liquid into the saucer with a quick release of his hairy thumb. "OK, put the lid back on and you are done for today."

"That was quick," I said.

"It will be quick until they multiply. Then we divide, transfer, divide, transfer, until the entire lab hood is full of one-liter colonies. It'll be plenty of work." Mr. Potter set the pipette back into a Pyrex beaker; the sound of glass-on-glass rang like a wind chime through the lab.

Carlton and I grabbed our backpacks and walked out into the quad. He immediately split off to the right, heading toward the baseball field.

"Hey," I called out.

Carlton stopped, looked back at me over his shoulder.

"I'm sorry about today," I said. "Sammy's a nimrod."

He nodded and turned away, ran straight into the sun.

Preston Goodman showed up at the old athletic shed every day at two o'clock wearing Easter-egg-colored Izod shirts, his collar turned up at the same angle as his perfectly Protestant nose. He'd laugh with Rocko while they both got stoned. Now that he was a regular at the shed, I'd backed off of my spying routine, skipping most of my locker and parking lot sightings. At the shed, I could get long looks at him. He shouldn't have been there—it was too dangerous for him, so much to lose. Whenever he showed up, I'd keep one eye split on him and the other on the access path from school, which probably made me look kind of crazed. Anyway, the day he wore a baby-girl pink Izod shirt, the one with a green—not black—alligator, he gave me a half nod in between tokes. A half nod—a monumental thing.

Tad, Walton's sole-source dealer and a mere sophomore, nudged me on the shoulder. "Hey, I think Prez likes you!"

"Shut up!" I reached for the nub of a joint in Tad's fingers.

"Nice blush you've got goin' there, Val," said Boxer, one of Tad's hanger-oners.

I coughed and with one big exhale sent a film of smoke up to the sky. I handed the roach to Boxer, who was already crimping open a metal clip. Once it landed safely in the clamp's jaws, I turned on my heels and headed up the path back to school, floating.

Carlton still hardly looked at me in bio lab, only turning to nod hello if Sammy wasn't there. But during our after-school punishment, he'd joke with me a bit, and when he smiled at me, his eyes shined. Partway through our punishment, I dropped an entire one-liter colony of fruit flies, about 25 percent of our work so far. Fruit flies spread all across the lab; they looked like tiny chocolate sprinkles on the white walls of the lab.

"I'm a complete moron, Carlton." I ran my hands through my hair, convinced there were a zillion fruit flies laying their eggs at the base of my follicles.

Carlton sprang into action, filling a beaker with acetic acid and an orange slice from his lunch bag, cutting a hole in the bottom of a paper filter and placing it on top of the beaker. "You're far from a moron, Val. Look."

Dozens of fruit flies flocked to the beaker, landed on the floating orange slice.

"Look at that. Fruit—attracting fruit flies." Carlton smirked. "Do you want to tell Mr. Potter about your remarkable scientific discovery, or shall I?"

"Holy crap! Did you just make a joke?" I fake-punched Carlton in the arm, and he grabbed my hand, pulled me into him for an awkward, congratulatory hug.

"You're smart, Val. Don't let anybody tell you different."

We ended up losing more than half a jar's worth of fruit flies, but Carlton quickly reassembled the rescued fruit flies and fed the rest of the colonies while I swept up broken glass.

Instead of his normal pattern of rushing to practice, Carlton waited while I grabbed my sweater and backpack. He held the lab door open for me. "I think we make a pretty good team, Val."

I recognized the look he was giving me—that same combination of bewilderment and fortune-telling I'd feel whenever Preston Goodman seemed to notice me at the equipment shed. False hope.

I slung my backpack over one shoulder. "With any luck, we'll get through this by next week."

Carlton's wide eyes squinted—it was as if he were crunching some exponential growth equations in his head. He let go of the door and swished away, didn't look back.

On our last day of detention, the liter jars were full with uncontrollable fruit flies. The penlight trick no longer worked effectively, and we lost dozens of flies during each transfer. They dusted the air like dandelion seeds.

"Congratulations you two," said Mr. Potter, surveying the rows and rows of jars in the lab hood. "You are free to go."

"All in all, that wasn't so bad," I said.

Carlton was already halfway down the aisle, aiming for his bat bag. He walked so fast, his parachute pants whistled.

"Got to get to practice. We've got the Hamilton game Friday."

"Are we gonna win?"

"If I can help it." Carlton looked sure and steady, like when he opened the jars of fruit flies. Unlike me, he was never afraid of the rush of bugs, tiny and fast, all seemingly aimed at teeth.

He was in the hallway before I could grab my backpack off the floor. "Wait up."

I wasn't sure if he heard me, or—if he'd heard me—that he'd still be there when I rounded the corner. But he stood outside the door, fiddling with his backpack's shoulder strap adjustments.

"Can I go with you?" I asked.

"To practice?" Carlton's voice cracked.

"Yes, to practice. Is that OK?" I felt dopey, like I was asking him to prom or something. He shrugged, then turned and headed outside.

"I take it that's a yes?" I said to no one, to myself, to the eddy of air formed by the rapid rubbing of Carlton's pants.

The rugby field was situated back to back with the baseball diamond. I figured if I played it right, sat at the top of the bleachers in between, I could pay enough attention to Carlton to seem interested and still get an eyeful of Preston.

Carlton stood on the mound throwing arcs and straight rocket pitches to Rocko. In between pitches, he'd rub his right cleat into the Carolina clay, puffing up crimson dust onto his Tide-white stretch pants. A few times I caught him looking up at me. It felt eerie, Carlton looking at me like he was a fruit fly and I was holding a penlight or a pipette of yeast. Would things be different if Carlton's nose were straighter or his pants didn't squeak or if he'd just look people in the eye? Impossible. I shifted my focus to the rugby field and searched for Preston.

The rugby field was a place of sheer mystery; the team's erratic movements baffled me. Guys clung together like a massive spider, the ball constantly in motion. I watched both fields like a slow game of ping-pong. The simplicity of what Carlton was doing lulled me; the secrecy of Preston's game made me exhale, until the tickle of my own breath forced me to turn my head toward baseball again. I was hooked. Rugby from the bleachers felt like legitimized stalking. I kept showing up at practice after practice. Sometimes Carlton would come over to me after he was done, and we'd walk off of the field together like we were actual friends.

Seventeen magazine had a timely article on how to get the one that's hard to get, a clever girl's guide to stalking. I read that article top to bottom, seventeen times. It seemed that the key to getting the out-of-reach guy was proximity to the target, coupled with either a tube or halter top. Seeing as it was early March and fifty-five degrees at best, I actively started working on a Plan B.

Macy's held the ultimate no-fail weapon in its clutches. I crossed the marble threshold and immediately felt out of place—hordes of lace, sequins in unmentionable places, over-engineered underwear. I managed to ignore the salesgirl, a watered-down version of Cindy Crawford, and made my way to the far back corner of the lingerie department where all things practical lived. There were bins of color-coded cotton panties. The walls were covered with bras made for mere mortals, devoid of tassels, metallic crystals, or any other hood ornaments. And in the middle of this organized normalcy was a half-mannequin, her chest lifted and artificially plumped with the object of my desire—the WonderBra.

"Isn't she beautiful?"

I turned around to see Cindy Crawford, who appeared to be glazed-over, mesmerized by the WonderBra.

"You should touch it," she said, lifting one of her skinny arms up to the mannequin's chest. She slid her fingers along the bottom of the cups. "It's super soft."

"That's OK," I said, moving backwards toward the cotton panty display. "I'm perfectly fine not touching her—I mean *it*, touching *it*."

Cindy Crawford looked at me like I was the freak and pulled her hand away from the mannequin. I waited until she rounded the corner back into the slut section before I ran back to the WonderBra display, snatching the first 32A I could find. I waited for the seclusion of my bedroom before I tried it on. There was no denying—it was a definite improvement. I think even the real Cindy Crawford would have admired the puffy results.

It was a perfect night for the Hamilton baseball game. There was a cool, low breeze, slow like Carlton's signature changeup. The stadium lights filled the field with artificial sun, a decent imitation of mid-day. Boxer and Tad waved me over, so I sat in the row right below them. The faint smell of Maui Wowie diffused from their clothes. I tried to talk to them, but they were in the middle of a serious baseball strategy discussion, battling over the merits of a line drive versus a well-placed bunt. A swarm of moths and random bugs hovered in the cone of stadium lights. I looked for signs of escaped fruit flies, even though I knew they'd be too small to see. Janice and Marcy, part-time stoners and best friends, drifted across the bleachers and sat down next to me. Both of them were just one facial feature short of being popular. Janice had inherited a largish Greco-Roman nose, and Marcy's pearly blue eyes were a little on the buggy side.

"Where are your team colors?" Janice asked me, pulling her Walton sweatshirt flat in front of her.

"Yeah," echoed Marcy. She was sporting team sweatpants with "Walton High" plastered up the sides.

"I've got all the team spirit I need in here," I said, thumping my chest with a fist, feeling the WonderBra's soft cushion.

"Here, have this," Janice said, handing me a "Walton #1" foam finger.

"You can point it at your boyfriend," Marcy said.

I looked around for Preston, wondering how Marcy knew my secret.

"Yeah, I heard you were dating Carlton," Janice said.

"Eeew! Where'd you hear that?"

Tad hit me on the shoulder. "Way to go, Val," he said. "But don't go leaving us for the jocks!"

"I am *not* dating Carlton!" I said, my voice cracking at the word "not." I remembered Sammy Springer, his gawky imitation of Klingon Carlton, the wet in Carlton's eyes.

Janice flicked her long, rusty hair over her shoulder. "If she did leave you stoners for a jock, I'd hope she'd at least upgrade from Carlton Spencer to someone with a normal head." Janice's rhino nose curled up at the mention of Carlton's name.

"Carlton's not that bad," I said. The roar of the crowd smothered my voice. Our Walton Wolverines took the field.

By the top of the fifth, we were beating Hamilton High, 2-0. Carlton looked strong; his arm fired pitches with precision. There had been no more *Valerie and Carlton sitting in a tree* speak since the second inning. I scanned the crowd for Preston. There was no sign of him.

Hamilton had runners on first and third with no one out. Rocko flashed hand signals to Carlton, and Carlton shook his head no to all of them. Finally, Rocko made a signal that made Carlton nod. He pulled the ball behind his back; ground his right foot into the mound. The ball left his hand like spitfire, shot toward the pocket in Rocko's glove. The ping of the bat connecting with the ball rang in my ears for endless seconds. The next sound I remember hearing was Carlton's sharp scream. He fell to the ground. One of his hands grabbed at his crotch while the other stretched out, reaching for the dead baseball. The first baseman ran in and scooped it up barehanded, throwing it—too late—across the plate to Rocko. Hamilton scored, and the crowd turned its full attention to Carlton. He'd twisted himself into a modified fetal position, rocked back and forth, moaning like a dying cat.

"Looks like you guys won't be having any children," Janice said.

Boxer and Tad were uncharacteristically silent. They were both grabbing at their own junk, some kind of male sympathetic reflex. I picked at the foam finger without even realizing it, releasing flecks of artificial snow all around me. The trainers took Carlton away, a coiled caterpillar on a canvas stretcher.

Walton got shelled and lost the game—8-2. Carlton lost a testicle, or at least that was the word in the hallway. He was out for a full two weeks, which was not nearly enough time for the jokes to die. Carlton had a slew of nicknames he didn't know about—Grapefruit Balls, Stinger, Cupless, to name a few. When Carlton walked back into biology lab, he looked even more pasty and thin than usual. I wanted to cocoon him, feed him orange slices, warm him with a penlight.

I couldn't help but look down at his crotch for some sign of disfigurement. His eyes caught me in the act. I gave him a weak smile, but he just pursed his lips.

Sammy Springer practically leapt off of his lab stool at the sight of Carlton. "Hey, welcome back, Twisticle!"

The whole class laughed, even me. I quickly reverted to a straight face, and waited for Carlton's retort. Nothing came, not even a glance. Carlton was as still as larva.

Carlton gave me a couple more weeks of the silent treatment. The rugby team was about to take on Hamilton High, and it had all of the feelings of a true revenge match. The Hamilton jackasses were all still revved up from the baseball victory. There were lots of Hamilton High letter jackets in the stands waving defaced Walton Wolverine dolls in the air. I sat alone on the sidelines on spurts of grass that were trying to germinate. I couldn't think of anyone I could ask to come with me. Rugby was too obscure for the burnouts; Janice and Marcy wouldn't have wanted to get their butts dirty out here on the field.

The game started without warning, no irritating cheerleader hullabaloo to greet Preston and his teammates. He looked great, even though he was wearing tall mustard socks. The field was full of grunts and loud smacks, and I tried to decipher their codes of movement. Watching from ground level, the players looked like an enormous circular centipede fighting for an oval egg. It made no sense to me, even having watched a dozen practices. Preston was everywhere on the field, but I had no idea if he was doing well or screwing up. But he was all I could see, forged steel legs, an ass that his teammates patted constantly.

"I didn't know you liked rugby." Carlton sat down next to me on the hard, cold ground. I hadn't noticed him in the crowd.

"Well yeah, kind of, after watching all of those practices."

Carlton laughed, but it came out like more of a snort. "I thought you were watching me."

"I did—I watched you too—I …"

"Stuff it. Who's winning?"

"I have no idea."

We looked at each other and laughed. Carlton's laugh was huge—I could see his molars. He reached over and pulled the hood of my sweatshirt up on top of my head, electrifying my hair.

"Do you even know the rules?" he asked.

We both looked up at the field. Preston was leaning over, adjusting a sock, and looking right at us. He smiled and gave me a partial wink. I bit down on the strings of my hooded sweatshirt, felt my saliva travel through capillary action down the heavy cords. Oh, Christ, he probably thought Carlton was my boyfriend.

"There's a Wolfpack party at Rocko's tonight," Carlton said.

"Wolfpack party?"

Carlton picked up a stick and scratched at the dirt by his feet. "Wolfpack—you know, all the sports teams.

Rocko's parents are gone. It's a kegger. If you want to go with me."

The fans around us screamed. Apparently Preston had scored, because his teammates were paddling his butt and smiling. I looked over to Carlton. "Absolutely."

Carlton offered to pick me up at my house, but I met him at the curb so it didn't turn into a meet-my-parents, date-y kind of thing. He looked nice—no parachute pants, but instead real, live jeans and a striped polo shirt. His car smelled like a mixture of cologne and sweat socks. We listened to Major League Baseball on the radio instead of talking, which seemed weird but OK.

As soon as we got to the party, Rocko tasked Carlton with driving across town to Rocko's cousin's house to scrounge up more vodka.

"Do you mind?" Carlton asked.

"Go. I'll be fine. Once I find the keg, that is."

I nodded at all kinds of people I'd never met and found my way to the keg of Busch Light. I sat down on Rocko's couch with a party cup half full of foam.

"Mind if I sit here?"

Preston appeared out of nowhere—apparently my stalking skills had dulled. He reached into the bowl of Doritos on the coffee table, and sat down next to me with a solid thud. I concentrated on the music, which was loud and unfamiliar. A thumpy, constant bass beat fed in through my feet like pulsing Jell-O.

I shouted to overcome the music. "Great game today."

Preston nodded, stuffing the crunchy triangles into his mouth.

I knew this was my chance to impress him, to keep him on the couch. "So what exactly is a hooker, anyway?" It sounded stupid the second it left my mouth.

"All those practices you watched, and you don't know the positions?"

I pulled the party cup up to my lips and swallowed hard. The malt and hops mixed in a confusing way on my tongue.

Preston looked at me with grass-green eyes. "I know that you watch me."

Beer sat in my mouth in a sour pool.

Preston arched his right arm around his back and rubbed his shoulder blades. "I'm a little sore after the game today," he said. "Any chance I could get you to give me a back rub?"

I remembered how to swallow. The warm beer tasted like medicine.

"Hey, Rocko," Preston yelled across the room to the foosball table. "Have you got a tennis ball?"

Rocko released a hand from the rod handle and pointed at the hall closet. The foosball table erupted with shouts, Rocko apparently giving up a goal. I looked around for Carlton, but he was nowhere.

"Come on," Preston said.

He grabbed my hand, pulled me from the couch. I tugged at the hem of my miniskirt with my cup hand and dribbled splotches of Busch Light behind me. The music changed—"Every Breath You Take" by the Police.

My Preston mantra. He walked me through the crowd, never letting go of my hand. I wanted to wipe that hand something awful—the combination of Preston and me was slippery.

The hall closet was a walk-in with large, double doors that opened toward us. It was obvious that Rocko's family was obsessed with jackets—puffy down vests, sport coats, slick yellow rain shells, with Rocko's Walton letterman jacket the prominent bookend. Preston freed my hand, and I brushed it over the baseball diamond patch on Rocko's sleeve. I thought about Carlton, shining Carlton, on the mound. He'd been so in control there, conducting the sound of the crowd with his changeups and fastballs. Until Hamilton.

"Here they are." Preston reached down to the corner of the closet and retrieved a silvery can of tennis balls.

"Can you hold my beer?" Preston handed me his cup and released the inner tab of the can with a "pfft." He peeled back the soft, aluminum lid, folded it into the shape of a potato chip. Rubbery air filled the closet.

"Hey, there's a couple in the closet!"

I looked out to the hallway—a guy wearing an "I'm with stupid" T-shirt pointed at Preston and me and then laughed with a toothy smile.

"Lock 'em up, Buzz," some lanky guy next to him said.

I felt the closet door push into my back, and I tried hard not to spill our beers on Rocko's coat collection. Preston let out a "Hey!" and pulled me toward him.

The closet went black.

"Well," said Preston, "this is an interesting situation." He placed a hand on the skin right above my hip bone. "Do you think you could tell me your name?"

"Valerie," I said, talking right through the darkness.

"Well, Val, how about that massage?" Preston reached around, found my hands, one by one, taking the party cups away. I could feel his body squat, hear the plastic scrape of the cups as he set them on the floor. His hair smelled like Ivory soap. "Grab a tennis ball from the can," he said.

"Where the heck is it? I can't see a thing."

"Looks like you're going to have to find things through touch."

Touch. Me. Touching Preston Goodman. *Seventeen*'s guide to successful stalking really hadn't covered what to do once you captured the target, let alone once you locked yourself away with him in a coal-dark closet. I could hear my own breath, shallow and rapid-fire. Preston probably thought I was on the verge of passing out, and maybe I really was. I reached out into the darkness, trying hard to keep my hand above waist height. I brushed the fabric of Preston's shirt. It was rough, like artificial turf.

"Cold," he said.

I moved my hand lower, a little more to the right.

"Getting warmer."

Preston moved a finger up and down the bare skin of my side. I pictured him as a Boy Scout—uniformed, starting a fire with a stick, a piece of flint and his hot, moist exhales. I swung wide and felt an arm. I pressed into it. Biceps. Holy Crap. Preston Goodman's biceps.

"Hotter, definitely."

I traced Preston's forearm down to its base, to the slick metal cylinder in his hands.

"Very good, Val. Now grab one."

I reached for the tube, but Preston tilted it into my belly. One of the rubbery balls landed on my midriff; I grabbed it and squeezed it as hard as I could.

Preston turned away from me and told me to rub the tennis ball up and down his back. I cupped the ball into my palm and rolled it up to his neckline and then back down again. When I traced Preston's scapula, he moaned out loud, and I could hear snickers from outside the closed door. *They're doing it!* someone yelled, probably Stupid guy. My palms were moist, and it seemed like the ball was getting heavier with my sweat. It skipped along the bunched-up parts of Preston's shirt, on the tiny humps of his vertebrae.

"That was great, Val," Preston said. "Now let me do you."

Could I die from being this happy? Preston glided the tennis ball across my back, only slowing when he reached some hollow spot, my lower back or the base of my neck. It was only then—with those deliberate, deep strokes—that I remembered to breathe. But as soon as I relaxed, inhaling and exhaling at a slow, even pace, Preston reached up underneath my blouse and started searching around. His warm hand slipped under the not-so-protective underwire of my WonderBra. Somewhere mid-grope, when Preston's nimble fingers managed to find a nipple, the closet door opened.

Carlton.

He looked at me, my chest expanding with beefed-up body parts, and then he looked at Preston. A curtain of blush rose up Carlton's neck like water climbing a paper towel.

Preston's hands flew off of me and I felt the quick-release front of my WonderBra snap wide open. I grabbed at my T-shirt and tugged it straight down, trying to return to normalcy. Preston slid out from behind me, past Carlton, into a wave of Duran Duran. "Sorry, man," he said.

Sorry man. So he did think Carlton and I were together.

"And to think, I was starting to worry about you," Carlton said.

"Carlton," I looked around for Stupid guy to explain, but he was gone. "We got locked in there. It wasn't … It was just …"

He looked away from me, down to the closet floor. "I guess that explains your sudden interest in watching practices."

I let go of my T-shirt, felt the WonderBra slide every which way. "I wanted to watch you, too, Carlton. I really did."

His eyes rested squarely on my chest. I looked, too. The miracle had clearly ended.

"If I'd known," Carlton stopped short, chugged the rest of his beer. His Adam's apple bobbed and bobbed.

I reached out and put a hand on Carlton's drinking arm, but he shrugged and my hand dropped. His eyes were as red as a wild-type fruit fly's. He crumbled his party cup and threw it on the closet floor.

I looked for Carlton later, after I'd restored my hair, miniskirt, and my chest to order in Rocko's parents' pink-and-white master bathroom. When I emerged, the party was in full throttle. Guys in striped polo shirts crowded the living room, none of them Carlton. Preston lorded over the foosball table, his arm wrapped over the naked shoulder of a Pat Benatar wannabe. I figured that was the last place Carlton would be.

I slid the patio door along its track, and it stuttered open to reveal the keg and its worshipers. Janice and Marcy were there—barnacles clinging to trash can punch. They didn't remember seeing Carlton and laughed at me through a haze of vodka when I told them about the closet incident. I couldn't laugh. Carlton's eyes were reprimanding ghosts.

His car. If Carlton's car was there, then I'd keep looking for him at the party. If his car was gone, I'd have to steal the keys from drunk-ass Janice or Marcy and drive us all home. I walked down the dark side path of the house, suffering the occasional scratch of a holly bush. The line of cars stretched far past the driveway. Halfway down the street I saw Carlton's GTO—lollipop red with white racing stripes, Walton's colors. His baseball cap sat on top of the hood. I grabbed it and felt the weight of his keys inside of it. He'd left a note inside of it too, but I had to climb in the car and turn on the dash lights to read it. The radio switched on when I turned the key. AM 620. Baseball radio. Twisticle radio. I was worse than Sammy Springer and his plastic head. Much worse.

> *V—Please bring car to school on Monday and leave the keys under the floor mat.—C*

A scratchy voice called out the one-two pitch in some faraway ballpark. *High and outside. Ball two.*

Sitting in Carlton's GTO felt wrong, like graduate-level stalking. I think even *Seventeen* magazine would have disapproved, made me sign an insanity waiver and give up my subscription. Still, I couldn't help myself from prying—it wasn't like Carlton made it easy to get to know him. The car was probably full of Carlton clues.

A Saint Christopher medal stuck out from the dash. Sunflower seeds littered the driver's-side floor. I ran my index finger between the driver's seat and the stick shift, poked repeatedly into the crevice. I pulled out half a stick of gum and a copper penny. A jumble of bat bags, ball bags, and orphaned athletic socks clogged the back seat. The whole car smelled a little like orange slices; I laughed, remembering the fruit flies. Carlton's confidence in me. *You're smart, Val.* No one ever told me that. Carlton. Crap—what other obvious clues had I missed?

Two-two pitch. Rollie really needs to get this one over the plate. Misses away. Ball three—full count.

I popped open the center console. Some guy named Zig Ziglar smiled back at me from the cover of a beat-up cassette tape. *Sell Your Way to the Top*. Unlikely I'd be getting to the top of anywhere, Zig, given my criminal trespassing tendencies. Plus being an all-around, complete ass to Carlton. But thanks for the vote of confidence.

It's a pitcher's nightmare—tie game. Bases loaded. Three-two pitch. Rollie's got his relief hands full tonight. But if anyone can do it, this former Cy Young winner's got the stuff.

I put Zig back into the console, sandwiched him between Pink Floyd and Judas Priest cassettes. Why did Carlton keep pothead music in his car? Did I really even know him in the slightest?

Rollie's looking a little flustered out there, folks. He's wiping his forehead … taking another grab at the rosin bag. Rollie's looking over at the bench, looking at Coach Bramberger for a sign.

I flipped the glove box open. A crumpled note fluttered onto the floorboard. I smoothed it out in my lap, surprised to see my name at the top. It was written in pencil, but half of the words were crossed out in big, smeary patches.

> *Val—*
> *I don't know how to tell you this, but I'm beginning ….*
> *BLOTCH. You probably don't …. BLOTCH. I*
> *hope …. BLOTCH. Let me know.—C*

I closed my eyes, pictured myself in some Major League ballpark. It's a night game. Carlton's on the mound. I'm up on the scoreboard platform and I'm pointing an enormous penlight right at him. He's ectothermic. He soaks all the light rays into himself as if they are fuel. There's no sweat underneath the band of his hat, no need for him to look to the dugout, to Coach. He doesn't need any signs. He knows exactly what to do.

Before I folded the note back up, I ignored the advice of *Seventeen* magazine to keep all missions covert and left a trace of myself—a moist, shimmery lip print, the softest of kisses—in the middle of the paper. I tucked the note under the driver's seat visor, imagined it fluttering onto Carlton's lap. His signature straight face, breaking just a touch. A light bulb moment. His smile.

I started the engine.

ACKNOWLEDGMENTS

Unending thanks to the team at Moon City Press, especially Michael Czyzniejewski, Joel Coltharp, Karen Craigo, and Cam Steilen for their hard work and dedication to this book and for making my born-in-the-stacks-of-my-childhood-library dream come true. Thank you, Shen Chen Hsieh, for designing the amazing cover.

Thank you, Kathy Fish, Christopher Gonzalez, William Haywood Henderson, Sara Lippmann, Kim Magowan, Michelle Ross, Tiffany Quay Tyson, Jennifer Wortman, and Tara Isabel Zambrano, for your kind praise and generosity of spirit. Special thanks to Kim Magowan and Michelle Ross for encouraging me to submit my collection to Moon City Press.

Thank you to my multitude of teachers over the years, especially Beth Alvarado, Andrea Dupree (you'll always be my first!), Michael Henry, Jennifer Itell, Suzanne Kingsbury, Erika Krouse, Karen Palmer, Chris Ransick, Amanda Rea, Jennifer Wortman, and especially to Kathy Fish, Jessica Roeder, and William Haywood Henderson. All of you are brilliant and have taught me so much about craft, and many also have emphasized the value of drinking good wine. Your collective wisdom floods me every time I sit down to write.

Thank you to all the editors who have given these stories homes over the years and who, in doing so, gave me the much-needed encouragement to continue writing. Special thanks to the tremendous editors who took their valuable time to help improve my stories and shape me into a better writer in the process: Tara Campbell, Ingrid Jendrzejewski, Kim Magowan, Jen Michalski, and Kaitlyn Andrews-Rice.

Thank you to my *Split Lip Magazine* family, especially Janelle Bassett, Anna Cabe, Maureen Langloss, Wendy Oleson, and Becky Robison, for their always-dependable cheerleading and open access to such incredibly talented editorial brains.

Speaking of brains, I have to thank my three brainiac older brothers for setting the bar so high, I had no choice but to try harder at everything. They continue to amaze me.

My thanks are beaming up to the heavens for the pure gift of my parents, Edward John Finn and Michelina Grace Cilea Finn. Dad taught me to see the beauty of science everywhere, right down to the table salt (we called it "NaCl" at the dinner table). Mom showed me by example that it's never too late to dedicate yourself to art. Between the two of them, both halves of my brain were equally encouraged to explore.

This book would not exist without the unselfish support of my husband, Karl. Thank you for always believing that my time spent in the "girl cave" writing is valuable and for encouraging all of my late-night, green-tea-fueled marathons.

The author would like to thank the editors of the following journals, where the listed stories have originally appeared:

The Adroit Review: "The Erratic Flight Patterns of Bats"
The Airgonaut: "What Remains"
Barrelhouse Magazine: "Stealing Baby Jesus"
Bartleby Snopes: "Adopting Mercy"
Bath Flash Fiction Volume 2: "Returning to Karakong"
(b)OINK: "Frat Party"
Boston Literary Magazine: "Darby, Nightfall"
The Conium Review: "DJ's Addictions"
theEEEL by tNY Press: "The Constant Nature of
     Toxicity"
Ellipsis Magazine: "Jericho Falls"
Fiction Southeast: "Plan B"
FlashBack Fiction: "Santo Spirito, 1577"
Heavy Feather Review: "Bounty"
Hobart, reprinted in *HAD*: "Three is a Rational Number"
Jellyfish Review: "Gravitational Waves"
jmww journal: "Word Search"
Lost Balloon: "Born Again" and "Grafton Hill"
matchbook: "Cruel Summer"
Moon City Review: "General Considerations of
     Independent Living"
MoonPark Review: "Birth Marks"
Necessary Fiction: "Lunar Facts"
Noble/Gas Quarterly: "School Lessons"
The Nottingham Review: "The Circumference of
     Everything"

MOON CITY
SHORT FICTION AWARD
WINNERS

2014
Cate McGowan
True Places Never Are

2015
Laura Hendrix Ezell
A Record of Our Debts

2016
Michelle Ross
There's So Much They Haven't Told You

2017
Kim Magowan
Undoing

2018
Amanda Marbais
Claiming a Body

2019
Pablo Piñero Stillmann
Our Brains and the Brains of Miniature Sharks

2020
Andrew Bertaina
One Person Away From You

2021
Michele Finn Johnson
Development Times Vary

9 780913 785737